CB

OLD LIBERTY

OLD LIBERTY

by Marshall Terry, Jr.

1961

NEW YORK · THE VIKING PRESS

FIRST PUBLISHED IN 1961 BY THE VIKING PRESS, INC.
625 MADISON AVENUE, NEW YORK 22, N. Y.

PUBLISHED SIMULTANEOUSLY IN CANADA BY
THE MACMILLAN COMPANY OF CANADA LIMITED

LIBRARY OF CONGRESS CATALOG CARD NUMBER: 61-7276

PRINTED IN THE U.S.A. BY THE COLONIAL PRESS, INC.

For freshmen

OLD LIBERTY

I

Chapter One

BO DUDDLEY was a one-eyed boy from a Hoosier place. He was a sincere, fine boy and he had God's biggest heart, and the thing about Bo Duddley was that it all fascinated him, and meant something to him, and he planned to write about it one day. He wasn't really one-eyed, he just couldn't see doodle-squat out of one eye. He said he saw through a glass darkly; and I guess he did.

I had seen Bo Duddley around the campus and in the dorm quite a bit, and he lived in a room not too far from me on Top Floor, but I didn't actually get to know him until after we had been at Liberty about a month.

One night I had been trying to study in the library and after it closed I was wandering around over the campus under the trees when all of a sudden I saw what I thought was this other boy from Texas that I heard had been having a little fun at my expense concerning how I never wore anything but jeans and moccasins, and my sideburns and all, and saying that I must be a real comedian because *he* had never seen anybody like that in Texas, and how it was clowns like me that gave his state a bad name and so on, and livening up quite a few parties on Low Floor with that kind of snaky talk. It all oozed back to me, and it kind of chapped my rear, if you know what I mean, and this guy was a little faggio from *Dallas*, for God's sake, and then I thought I saw him coming down the path.

This kid I had in mind was a prissy boy with a block of hair he was always combing, and he wore these blackrim creep glasses and played the piano for them on Low Floor, and he did look *kind* of like Bo Duddley, and it was night, but there was a moon, and I thought it was him.

Then I was suffering from a pretty good case of the reds anyway, and so exploded down the path to this boy before I thought about it much, and popped him a good one in the stomach.

He sat down doubled up on the gravel, gasping, and sat there for about five minutes, and I saw then right away I had made a mistake and it wasn't that Low Floor boy at all.

It was old Bo Duddley.

Well, I apologized my head off, and I kneeled on the path by him apologizing and clapping him on the back.

And he started in to laughing, but he had to quit, and he still couldn't breathe so red hot, and had a look on his face like everything inside him was broken.

Finally I helped him to stand up, and I kept on saying how sorry I was, and he said he was all right, and I insisted we go up to my room, that was one of the only singles on Top Floor, and he inhaled his insides together and let me pull him up there.

In the room I opened the big closet doors and rolled out my bar, and got him to swallow down some Jack Black, and I sipped some too, and pretty soon he was breathing just fine and we had passed a happy night talking and it was getting light outside. Bo Duddley and I ended up good buddies that night.

He was the first one I had invited in to my room, and the first real friend I made at the college.

We told each other things, and I guess we were both homesick because he talked mostly about his family, and he had a sister too, Margie, and he talked about how he was going to be a writer when he got to rolling in the world and, come to think of it now, I mostly listened and Bo Duddley did the talking. He loved to wander on and talk, and he loved a lot of things, and was a pretty intense kind of a boy, in his funny, poky way.

"Aren't you an Iota legacy?" he said. I said I was, my Daddy had been in that fraternity here at Liberty, but I had told them to leave me alone at the beginning of school and hadn't joined. Bo Duddley was the head of the Iota pledge class and that night he worked on me to join.

After that we went around together, and were friends, and I even let him borrow the T Bird, and I wouldn't do that but for Bo and Little Dick.

We agreed that Liberty College, throw in Olive Hill next door, was pretty much the ass end of the universe, as far as anything to *do* went. Only Bo said being at Liberty College was like living on top of the moon during a lunar eclipse. That was the way he liked to express things.

It wasn't all that bad, of course. Bo loved the studies, and I liked Liberty all right, you could do what you wanted if you made the grades.

Liberty is this little college that is I don't know how many hundred years old in the woods of old Pennsylvania. My Daddy graduated from it, and Bubba went for a year, so I came up too, it was in the family to do it. Like I say, the college was right outside the two-bit town of Olive Hill, where

5

they had a cafeteria and a movie and a roller rink and a hotel and stores and all kinds of exciting things, such as the mop-handle factory.

They hated us in Olive Hill.

There were more kinds of different boys at the college than I had ever seen. Some of them were very great, and some were a bunch of outfits and either studied *all* the time, and would sleep in the library, or played cards and drank and fooled around, and some drank too much, or took to being queers or gambled, and like that.

Bo Duddley was one of the great boys there, and Harmon Baumberg, that would hang bolognas that his mama sent him in his socks out the window and rage around when I stole them, and Abraham Lincoln Guznik, that wanted to be a poet, and Little Dick, who lived down at the end of our hall, and kept Horsehead in there with him. None of them was anything, that is, fraternity, except Bo, but there were a lot of fraternity boys in our part of Top Floor. Slugger was up there, a tall suavo that would wear brass-button jackets; and Smoke Smith, that was a real snowman that had been kicked out of Harvard besides Princeton; and Rojo, a bright, bandy-legged little swinger, and they were all Iotas, and Smoke Smith was the president.

All the boys in the college lived in this one big stone monster of a dorm, Old Liberty. The fraternity boys mostly lived on Top Floor and on Low Floor and had their suites and club rooms there, and the GDIs and the real serious spooks and birds and most of the boys of that nature lived in the middle floors between, and they called that part the Womb.

There wasn't too much to Liberty College. Old Liberty was the biggest thing about it.

That dorm was the ugliest Goddamn thing I ever saw and I got so I loved it living in it. Bo Duddley loved it too, because it was so old and massive and hideous. Outside, Old Liberty

6

loomed up like some huge prehistoric monster hunkered up on its haunches. It was kind of silly looking, outside. It was a mass of thick black walls with big oakwood doors, and real tall leaded windows, four stories; and at each corner was a high old tower, and each one had a tremendous round window, looking from the lounge rooms up there, like four Cyclops eyes staring at you. A little domed observatory sat on the center roof; but nobody went up there any more to look at stars. Still, when twilight would come brushing over the campus, with all the big old oak and elm and maple trees along the paths whispering in the wind and with the sun catching the tips of the trees to yellow and orange and red, and all the ivy looking like blood on the walls, Old Liberty looked lovely.

Inside, it was a mess. It smelled kind of like the armpit of some old boy you're wrestling, or like a jock that's been left hanging in a locker room for two or three years. It was all dark wood halls and dim lights and splintery floors, and most of the faucets hummed tunes and the hinges were mostly undone on the johnny seats. The rooms were huge and comfortable, though, and I kept thanking the Lord I had one to myself. Bo Duddley had to room with that poor alcoholic bastard Monroe Gee, and I didn't know how he stood to be in a room with him. The room had a rotten sock-and-gin stink so bad Bo had to keep a big thing of Airwick in there all the time and the windows wide open even in a blizzard, and every night about 2 a.m. in the morning here comes Monroe Gee staggering along the path to Old Liberty singing,

"Old Bo Duddley is a dirty son of a bitch,
Old Bo Duddley is a dirty son of a bitch"

to the tune of the "Battle Hymn of the Republic," and then Bo would get up and undress the poor pimple-face drunk and tuck him in the sack. Bo took Monroe Gee as his kind of per-

7

sonal albatross and stuck up for the two-bit scoundrel and never seemed to mind a bit. And I suspect Monroe Gee loved Bo.

Well, after we came to be friends both me and Bo broadened out a little more. He had me to go around with some of his fraternity buddies and would set it up for them to hotbox me, and helped them rush me pretty hard again. And Bo got to know Harmon Baumberg and Little Dick and some of the boys I knew, so he came to realize his wonderful roommate wasn't the only living specimen of a non-fraternity boy. It was good for both of us, but he kept chipping away at me to join his club, and I kind of softened to it, because I thought if my Daddy and Bo Duddley were Iotas, it must be pretty good.

Anyway, that is one reason I want to write this down, because of all those boys and especially for the sake of Bo Duddley, I know Bo would like it that I was doing it. That is part of it, and another reason, of course, is Vera.

How I met Vera is strange, and kind of like meeting Bo, except with Vera it was more that I was the one got hit.

It was in the cafeteria in Olive Hill, sometime in October.

I went in there one evening. I was tired of the same old gravied meat and mashed potatoes at the college and of sitting in the school dining hall where you had to sing every two minutes in the middle of your dinner.

I take my time in a cafeteria line and won't be rushed along and scared into saying that I'll take something that you tote to your table and just sit and stare at and couldn't eat to save your soul. When I got to the trays, the salad girl was already yelling to me, "Salad order, please?" When I took a wilted salad the meat girl was yelling to me, shoving that spade she had back and forth through a slop of horrible hash. I took the roast beef, it didn't look too terrible. Vegetables were harder, and I stopped there for a long time, holding up the line. They didn't carry okra or little green onions or red beans or blackeye peas, or any vegetables that you would care to eat especially, but that wasn't my trouble. I had seen this girl.

My eyes kept going down to the next stop in the line, next to bread and drinks and the cashier, and I was hung up there staring at the dessert girl. Finally I edged along and gawked at the desserts and at last I looked up and stared straight at her, and *inmediatamente* the Great Golden Horny Bird came swooping down and dug its claws in me and I heard the Cry. But, it was more than just that, too. It absolutely halted me, and I stood there in the line full of the strangest feelings, all sorts of strange feelings, like I was being all over sandpapered with velvet.

Because she looked so strange and lovely there, and she shouldn't of been there, in that cafeteria, just a little, short girl, in her white outfit that was so clean, her black hair straight as a whip on her head, not wearing any makeup, and her eyes flat and full of absolutely nothing.

She said, "Dessert order, please?"

She never flicked her eyes looking at me, as if I wasn't goggling at her, and then I looked down again and saw she had ripe red cherry tarts and soft pink rhubarb pies and dark chocolate cake and long creamy-looking eclairs. And I bolted on to the cashier, and never had any dessert at all.

After dinner there was a Western on at the show, then Dutch's lured me in. It was where the Liberty boys went to drink beer and pick up the dollies. I sat in there, with the Golden Bird perched on my shoulder, and spent an hour just peeling the labels off cool beer bottles. They slipped off like decals, and my mind kept slipping away with them back to that girl. I began the old routine and tried to pick up a false redhead, but she was a giggler and I got tired of her and let her go. And I went back to Liberty, and asked different guys

9

about the dessert girl at the cafeteria. One of them told me it was Vera, and I got the story on her; and I was wild just to talk to her, but it was a long time before I ever did. It was so strange, I'd known a million girls.

Looking back—God knows, it hasn't even been a year in time—I want to tell this most because of Bo and because of Vera. They are the main reasons, except for me. I want to tell it for my sake, too. So much happened, in just that time. And one thing I keep remembering besides all this, and it really seems ten million years ago, was the day I left Javalina to come to Liberty. That is very clear, and I keep remembering it, though the boy in the picture hardly seems like me.

We had had rain in the spring, and the summer hadn't been too bad, and by fall, on the day I left, there was still green grass. The sky stretched out tight and far, so blue it hurt to look at it, and the sun was shining on the white chalk cedar hills.

Our river cut like a blessing through our land: it all had never been so beautiful.

My family stood out in front of the Big House to say goodbye. The wind blew up little bursts of white dust, but it was cooler than it had been. They were in a kind of solemn circle around my car, that was loaded down so the rear end drooped. Nobody said much for a minute, but waited for it to be time for me to go.

Then Mama came and kissed me, and my sister, Aglaia. I said goodbye to Bubba. Uncle Sweet nearly tore my hand off in his quick old grip, and he didn't speak, but he never told you what he meant in words. He had come up from Mexico to say goodbye.

Grandmama had come out of the house, on canes hacked out of hard twisted wood. I kissed her. She had Pedrito give me the big can of laxative she had for me, and she told me not to mind taking some if the Yankee food clamped down on me.

Daddy came over then and we said goodbye.

"I know you'll do fine," he said.

"Yes, sir," I said.

"Well," he said, "you don't have to stay up there, you know."

"Goodbye, Daddy," I said.

"*Hasta,* Redwine."

I scrunched down into the sweet new T Bird and speeded off, waving my hat, and tried to give a yell for them, but it came out kind of a silly little squeak, and I drove on along the *sendero* and slowed down for the first of the beautiful creaking pushgates and got to going slower and slower until I reached the highway; then I cracked her down and flew up that highway north, going 900 miles an hour, but I thought my heart would break.

And on that trip, driving to Liberty, I remembered something that my Daddy says that his father told him that came from my Great-Uncle Walker, who fought at the mission-fort at Bexar: a man is a strange sort of animal. A real man worships God, and he doffs his hat to a lady. He will get down on his knees in the mud to help a little child. He looks you square in the eye, and asks no quarter. At times he needs to cry, and he shouldn't be ashamed to do it.

And I wondered, going up to that college so far away, if I really needed to learn so much beyond what was in that saying from my Great-Uncle Walker, back then. All that is true, you know. But there were things I had to learn.

Chapter Two

ONE MORNING when I had waked up right at dawn and stood at the long narrow window in my room and watched a little smudge of sun on the rim of creation spread out, kind of nervous and not sure of itself, until the black and gray over the campus had merged into a soft color of earliness, and I had risen up singing, and the hell with the rest of them sleeping their lives away in that big bleak dormitory, I traipsed on down the hall to Bo's room where he was sleeping like always with his head under the pillow and wrenched it off and dragged him down and slung him under the shower, and let that hot drenching bliss come pouring over me, and sang again, until Harmon Baumberg came into the head, like he did, and asked if I would rather do that than sing.

"What's the matter?" Harmon said. "You couldn't find a bright towel?"

And Bo and I got dressed and walked down the solid dark wood stairs to the first floor and out the big front doors of Old Liberty and down the stone steps to the path. It was a glorious fall day, and the sun was coming up for real now. We walked by one gray or red building after another and by some ball fields and the chapel, by the auditorium and past the library, and so toured the college. We ate our cold eggs and toast on tin trays in the dining room, and drank hot coffee, and I ate one of Bo's eggs, and then even though it was pretty nippy we headed out into the woods for a walk, and finally sat on the bank of the little stream that ran along there in the woods.

That was in November, on the day I pledged Iota.

We didn't talk, but sat there for a while, in the early morning-time.

At last Bo said, "You up on the Humanities, Redwine?"

"No, Bo. I ain't hardly past Thucywhatsis. Who can read so much?"

"I think it's great," Bo said.

"It's great if you go for it. I read all I can of it, Bo, for dear Professor Finch. But it's like having a fine furry little rabbit in your hand, or something, when you're doing the reading, and then soon as I lay the book aside, it kind of hops away, and there's nothing much there, except maybe a pellet or two."

"Get serious," he said. "I think it's real rewarding, all the old plays and the poets and philosophers and the Hindus and Chinese and John Milton. It's tremendous, to me."

"Well, if I tried to read all the real tremendous things that the old boy assigns, I'd read my eyes out."

We were studying hard then; the courses got to be pretty hairy, you had to hump to pass them.

Bo considered that about reading your eyes out, and I could see it appealed to him.

"Milton read himself blind," he said. "But if you could be that fine a writer, it would be worth it."

"Now you get serious, hoss. Not to *see*?"

"He saw with an inner eye, Redwine."

"Fine. I guess that's why he never saw anything but dark stuff, then."

"He was great writer," Bo said. "You should read *Samson Agonistes* sometime, about how it is to be all bottled up and blind."

Then I let him tell me about John Milton, kind of like he

was the pieman and we two were going to the Fair. That was when Bo was in his Spicer phase, spending most of his time in the library, reading all this bother he thought he should know so he could cock his head back and mouth phrases and put on, because old Spicer told him that was the thing. Spicer was Bo's cousin, he was a sophomore. Bo had carried a book to breakfast and dipped his nose in it while I ate his egg, and now he opened it and reached it over to me, with his finger on a poem. It was about how old Buffalo Bill had died, and what a dude he was and all what he used to could do, and the end of it, where he had his finger, asked old man Death if Buffalo Bill was such a great dude now. It was the old Ozymandias idea, you know.

"Say," Bo said, "isn't that the greatest?"

"That is fine," I said. Poetry always struck Bo, especially when it was about dying.

The little stream skipped by us and the water swirled around on the stones at a narrow place making all the delicate little colors. I put my hand down into the coldness of the stream, and I didn't really care to talk Milton, or about being blind, or dying, much.

I said, "Are you planning to bring your girl in to the Spring Retreat?"

Old Bo was being awfully loyal to this old girl friend of his in Indiana, and I wished he could afford to bring her to the big spring weekend, that was supposed to be the most tremendous affair of all time, and was the only time most of them at Liberty had an actual date.

"I don't know," he said. "I hope so. Are you asking June? Some of them are bringing girls from almost as far."

"I don't know," I said. "Maybe not."

June was writing me from Javalina, and I had let Bo see some letters from her; but there were some others down there

14

I would rather of brought up for the Spring Retreat. Or right here. I never mentioned Vera, though.

"If you weren't such an ass," Bo said, "you'd join the group, and we could have a great time Spring Retreat with the Iotas."

"Believe I will," I said.

Bo leaped up and almost fell into the stream. "Hey, let's go tell the boys," he says.

So we did, and they were all happy, since Daddy had been a pretty big Iota in his day, and had passed along a little money since, and they gave me the gold and blue button and told me to come on to their party Saturday night, and we would celebrate. I hadn't known that I was going to join, really, until I said it, and I never had felt before that I needed a bunch of boys to tell me what to do, but after I had said it and got the pledge button I was glad, and I wired my Daddy, and hoped he would be happy too.

On Saturday night I danced a little jig in my room and made a face at myself in the mirror and went down the hall so I could go to the party with Bo Duddley. He was just dressing.

Monroe Gee was sitting on Bo's bed listening to Bo's hi-fi.

"What say," I said. I sat in the big leather chair that felt and smelled like the dentist's waiting room in Javalina.

Bo took one of those dead flannel suits from the closet, and he got out a tie of Liberty blue. He put on black and yellow Argyle socks, and changed his bucks for a pair of cordovans. Bo was all for it. He got his button from the dresser and screwed it into the buttonhole of his left lapel. Monroe Gee was sitting on the bed smoking cigarettes. The music was low: blind Shearing chords.

"Going in to town tonight?" Bo said to his roommate.

Monroe Gee threw his burning butt on the floor so Bo had to go over and heel it out. Monroe looked like a long tall skull; he had black hair that got kind of violent on him and bushy black eyebrows growing together straight over his nose. He had these sizable pimples on his face that when he got excited and started his foul-mouthed cursing got all red and purple at the edges and it seemed like their yellow pus-points wanted to pop. He elbowed down to the side of the bed and reached under and hauled up a gin bottle. When he drank from the bottle his throat reminded me of the way turkey-gobblers do right after they have been pecking at spoiled tomatoes.

"How about a drink, sports?" He offered it to me, then Bo.

"I would rather take a drink from a toilet," I says.

Bo gave me a look and went over and grabbed the gin and took a little pull.

"Attaboy," Gee said. "Drink up, sport, and be somebody. *Say,* swell. Or did we tongue it, big frat man?"

"Okay, hoss—"

"Okay, Redwine. What the hell, Monroe?"

Gee sat on the bed and scratched at the rotten crotch of his corduroys. I got tired of the odor of feet and smoke and gin and Airwick and went out in the hall and down to the head. Little Dick was there. He looked like somebody's kid in there. He was in his robe, and he had a brand-new dopkit with his initials on it in gold. He was waiting for Horsehead to get finished taking a crap.

"I hear you pledged," he said.

"Yo."

I didn't know what to say to him. He was a colored boy, and I liked Dick a lot. So I said why didn't he take the T Bird and take Horsehead to a flicker in town, it was a gay musical. I gave him the keys. And walked back to Bo's room thinking about Little Dick. On the first morning of school I had seen him, in the dining hall, and I thought he was serving. I scraped some eggs on my tray, then he gets some eggs, and he sits down next to me at the table and reaches over and shakes my hand very polite and tells what his name is and then starts lapping it up. For a while I sat there and couldn't eat. But Daddy always says to ask if you want to know, so I did.

"I guess you're in school?"

He grinned at me, eating eggs.

"Well," I said. "I didn't know, you know. I mean, I think that's fine." Then I ducked my head and tore into them eggs.

It turned out, too, that kid was one of the best old boys I ever saw, I don't care what color. I was glad he smiled when I handed him the keys.

So me and Bo Duddley went on down the hall and crossed over into real Iota territory.

Chapter Three

OVER THERE a bunch of the Iota boys were stationed around a pony in the hallway. They drank the beer from 18-inch mugs that had gold and blue crests. Slugger, all straight-jacketed in a coat buttoned three times in front, was at the tap. They came to meet us and herded me and Bo to the keg. Old Slugger foamed over a glass for us. All the boys sang,

> "Here's to Brother Walker, Brother Walker, Brother Walker,
> Here's to Brother Walker, he's with us tonight!
> He's with us—
> He eats it!
> He's with us—
> He eats it!

Here's to Brother Walker—
He's with us tonight!"

Then they sang the same for Bo. It made you feel great.
I drained that glass and got it filled up again. More boys
came along, and we sang to them and had some beer. The old
cheeks got to tingling, and I commenced to feel pretty good.
Pretty soon they led us through some double doors into the
Iota suite. It was like going into a furnace.

We went in there, and I shook a lot of hands and nodded
quite a bit at everybody. I could have a brew or two and get
to be a real good nodder. I saw some boys from Low Floor
and some other boys I never knew existed. Nobody was there
from the Womb, they wouldn't let them in. Bo and me and
some other pledges stood at the side of the den room and
clamped our feet in the ratty stained carpet and somebody put
an iced glass of bourbon in my hand. Bo and the others had
on dark suits and Oxford shirts and striped Liberty ties and
gleaming shoes, and the pledge button in the lapel; and I wore
mine in a hole of my belt in my jeans. We stood there and
watched the people.

The bourbon made me dizzy, and a little sick. It was raw
and cheap, not like the good Jack Black. But I was never so
happy in my life. In a while I proceeded straight across into
the noise and the folks, mingling with them over by the fireplace. The fireplace went all across the room, and it was full
of fire, good hard maple logs and apple logs in there and it
surely did smell sweet. I backed off and saluted the big red-
tongued Bull, rearing up with its hooves on the blue-gold
crest, over the mantle. It was breathing out fire and glory,
and was the symbol of the fraternity.

Then I floated in and out, and met folks, and laughed, and
had a good time, and I was going to find me a partner for a
hat dance or a Paul Jones, but then I saw Vera over there,

18

and I stopped and drank the whole glass down and stood chewing on the ice.

Somebody dragged me off. Smoke Smith had hold of me.

"Here, boy," he said. "Come with me. You like this party? It'll do, huh? You'd say it'd do, huh? Screw the books one night, huh? Going to get you a mug, there, Redwine, soon's you initiated. Come on here. You know your old man helped give this den? Huh? Sure you did. Yeah. Give a whole wad of money—some of them did, whole mess of old fools, fifteen years ago, I bet, since they did. Goddamn hole. Huh? Come on. Hey, Vera, how you, sweetie? Hoo? Doing all right? Say are? Yeah, gal. Being treated all right? You know you can come back to the old dad any time— Here, boy . . ."

Smoke Smith bucked me through the mob to the bar. He was the real dog of Liberty, a four-point man, his life was dedicated to nicotine, rye whisky, and the history of the Middle Ages, and he was the president.

He shouted at me, "Hey, 'fore long, you'll be a neophyte. Huh? Ain't no more fun than that. Is it, Rojo?"

Rojo made a kind of an uncomplimentary gesture to him.

Smoke had Rojo give him a mugful of rye and starts off into the crowd, and I started in there, but he realized how bad we would miss him and comes back.

"You just ask Rojo, Redwine. See? He knows. Some day Rojo going to give out of his supply and we going to depledge him. Say what?"

Rojo's old man kept the machines in the rest rooms well stocked, and Smoke Smith had a lot of fun with that.

"See old P.J. and the lads got their instruments out— no, there, Slugger, you sweet precious one, don't get excited, I don't mean that, instruments. Listen, boys, can't P.J. go that fiddle? Sure he can, pledges dear."

Smoke Smith stood in my path, clutching a cigarette, wild-eyed and elegant, and he had that mugful of hot raw rye, and drank me a toast to my Daddy, that had given money for this Goddamn hole of a party room, and finally he went off, yelling back, "Yeah. Your daddy would be proud, Redwine. Hey, there, P.J. . . ."

I saw that Vera was over with some other women. They were pretty old, 22 or 25. They were Mrs. P.J. and some old girls that went with the initiates.

I went to where P.J. was by the piano, cutting at his fiddle. Rojo came over, and got on his guitar. Somebody was three-fingering the piano, making thumbtacked music that would of been nice for an orgy. I put my arm around Bo Duddley, and he was singing all the songs. All I could hear was the Cry.

She looked good to me. She never talked to the other women, and she never smiled at the boys she talked to. She had on a green sweater and a black skirt. She came to the piano and we looked at each other. Her strange eyes kept flat and her lips were orange.

She stared at me and I turned and shook Bo's shoulder and asked him how he was making it. He was a little gone.

"There once was an Indian maid
Who said she wasn't afraid. . . ."

P.J.'s fiddle screeched. A thing was sitting at the piano playing it by slashing skinny hands up and down on the keys. It was old Simple Sampson, the idiot of the History department, he partied with the boys. He wore a jacket with an orange and black tiger leaping from its back. He was out of his mind. Smoke Smith pushed in by me and shouted and sang and patted me with a yellow-stained hand. They all shrieked out the songs.

"But much to her surprise
Her belly began to rise. . . ."

20

I leaned on the piano by Bo. Vera moved away. It was a black glossy old piano top and I put my mug down on it carefully because I was pretty sure it was made out of glass.

When I looked around later all the women were gone. I cut out, and went very slowly down the long dark stairs, outdoors.

Out there I leaned against the wall of Old Liberty, and the stone was cold and rough on my back. There was a moon and stars and some ice, and that was the story of the night. Outside I talked and sang to myself, and listened to the trees, and I wished I could see myself.

I went back up and it had got quiet.

Slugger had taken over the piano and was playing some cool, majestical stuff. Turk Randy, the neanderthal, was throwing empty bottles at the Bull over the fireplace. Rojo was laid out on a couch picking out sad sounds on his guitar. Bo was up on a table giving us Mark Antony. Two guys were wrestling in some glass on the floor. Somebody was racked out on top of the bar. A leg was busted off a chair, and a beautiful black German mug was smashed on the carpet.

Big Turk Randy came and put his hand on my shoulder, so we stood leaning back and forth at each other, like the rubber men you try your punch on at the fair.

"There isn't any rye left," he says. He looks like he wants to cry.

"Take my car, pledge," he says, "and bring back one thousand cases of rye."

"Yo," I said.

Turk Randy gave me the keys. He threw a bottle at the guy on the bar. He was a Low Floor guy.

Smoke Smith came in the den. "P.J. gone off in his wagon. Huh? Redwine? P.J. going to be in a haystack again?"

"God knows. Mr. Randy wants me to get some rye."

"Hell," Smoke Smith says, looking at Turk Randy. "Screw P.J. P.J. can take care of self, I guess. Huh?"

They left. All the old guys seemed to have gone off.

Bo Duddley and I stood arm in arm. "I come to bury Caesar not to praise him," Bo says.

"What's with the hegira down the hall?" Rojo says.

In a minute he comes back, rolling his eyes.

"P.J. is back," he says. "They have the Whale down there."

"Say," Bo says. "The Whale."

"Can we go?"

"Uhn-uh. Just the initiates."

I cursed.

"Sest la vee," Rojo says.

"What's she like?" Bo asked.

"I should know," Rojo said. "A whale."

"Wise guy," Bo said, and we took Randy's old hearse and headed into Olive Hill. I slammed over that bad road at the speed of light. We have some bourbon, but they have got the Whale. We drank the bourbon in gulps that didn't even burn and sang "Christopher Columbo." Until the car stopped, in the big middle of town, out of gas, and we had to walk three cold miles back to Liberty.

We stood on the road a while and saw that the stars were bright, cut clear as diamonds in the night. Then I mostly carried Bo back to the campus, Rojo walking silent as death behind us.

When we got back it was late. The suite was empty. There was a stink of stale beer and whisky and of some puke by the bar. There was no buzz left. We sacked old Bo out on the couch. Rojo lay down on the stained carpet and plunked some chords on his guitar.

> "On . . . the shore . . .
> They spied . . . a whore . . .
> Off came coats . . . and col-lars . . ."

"Come on," I said. We grabbed a load of bottles from the basket in the hall and took them to Smoke Smith's room. He was snoring, happy as sin. We covered him from feet to chin with bottles, and tiptoed out. I would of liked to be there when he waked up.

We sat in the stinking party room. Bo was in another world. We waited for the sun to come up. The fire was all burned down to ashes and bits of logs, and it was cold in Old Liberty.

"Congratulations, old Iota," Rojo said.

"Go screw yourself," I said.

He sang over and over and over:

"The eyes of Texas are upon you. . . ."

"Goddamn," I said. "I hope not."

Chapter Four

I THOUGHT Xmas was never going to come.

We had to study like a fool, and I fought my classes to a standoff, and kept wanting to go in to the cafeteria in Olive Hill, and even heard Vera had asked about me, but I never did, but plunged into doing things with Bo and Rojo and the Iotas.

We went to some of the towns and cities near the college and 100 or 200 miles away, and went one time to this co-ed college up in New York State, and there was 25 feet of snow up there. We had heard they had these fabulous parties, but when we got there I drew this Green Mountain girl for a date, and I had to keep my hat on to be as tall as her, and she thought she was the Virgin Goddess of the Hunt or something, but she was only frigid. We went to this great party where they played Sunday-school games and bobbed for *apples,* I swear to God. They were all real Eastern type boys up there, from Yale and those nests, and I finally had to tell one to quit bobbing for Bo's date.

We ranged around and had some good times, though. Thanksgiving I went home with Monroe Gee (he took old Bo, and Bo made me come along) and saw New York City, which thrilled Bo quite a bit but it bugged me. Gee got us some dates, three of them, but I never did luck on to a Gentile girl, and all these girls in New York City could say was "Oh yeah?" or "So what do you know?" and I mean, that got old.

Anyway, we did a few things so I wasn't completely miserable, and I rode the books pretty hard, but I was ready when December 18 rolled around.

Bo's cousin Spicer was going to take us home with him to Cincinnati, Ohio, to the cotillions and the comings-out, and Bo said he always went there for a week Xmas, said it was fantastic.

Bo worried a little about how I would do in that scene, I guess, because he kept explaining how it was all formal, and I told him I knew how to do.

The morning that we left I had to go to Russian class, or it was double cuts.

"*Cock Pashyvyatsay?*" Professor Bielo spit at me. "So you have join us, Mr. Valker? How nize."

Professor Bielo was a White Russian, and he was a mullet, and the only prof I really didn't like. He was a royalist and I always figured old Bielo was one good reason the Russians rose up against the Czar back there and that he must of had quite

24

a hand in suppressing the people until when he quit old Mother R. to come over to Liberty College and suppress poor ignorant freshmen like me that had enough trouble with Spanish in high school.

Bielo had this wonderful way of teaching, which was to shout something you didn't understand at you and then come stand breathing heavy over you so you could smell everything but the answer on him and see his gold and black teeth and his eyeballs that were bloodshot clean through the pupils.

"Fine," I said. "Just fine."

"In Russian, Mr. Valker," he screamed. "In *Russian*. I'm told you how many times ? Yesss? Mr. Speetzer?"

And he rattled on with it. It always took three centuries for his class to be over, he fixed the bell. If he hadn't scared me so bad I could of answered once in a while. Michael Spicer, who was a real bird even if he was Bo's cousin and we were going home with him, was his little darling pet. Bielo picked on me, and always in that stupid classroom with the Goddamn chalk dust boiling around up my nose I would wish for a brilliant command of the Russian language so that I could be able to think of ways to come back at him. I even memorized the Russian for "How is your wife?" but to say that would of been mean. Old Bielo had married this little young girl from town and brought her to live in one of the houses the faculty had on campus and then he had been kind of sorry. Mrs. Bielo, being about 18 years of age, and waking up to find herself with a tough dried-up old man that couldn't speak English much at all and I guess would shout *Cock Pashyvyatsay?* at her every time he came home for dinner and try to teach her Russian when that was not exactly what she was most keen after, Mrs. Bielo started being a dorm mother for the whole Low Floor. Mrs. Bielo was for the fraternities on Low Floor more or less what the Whale was for them on Top Floor, only she sneaked around where the

Whale didn't give a damn. I had never really met Mrs. Bielo but an old boy downstairs told me it was fine as wine in the summertime. I wouldn't really ever of said that particular phrase to old Bielo. He wasn't such a bad old fool, I guess, and I was sorry for him, considering Mrs. Bielo. It was just he bugged me so bad in class.

Michael Spicer and Bielo talked back and forth for about fifteen minutes chewing the fat in Russky about the fact that Alexander Sergeevich Pushkin was writing when Russian literature was under the influence of French literature and that old Push is read more than any other Russian poet (I know he was read more by *me*) and such jazz as that, which Professor Bielo later condescended to tell us about in murdered English. Then the old boy launched off on a new monologue. It was about some two-bit novel the class had to read by some very famous character we have all heard of, M. I. Lermontov. I figured M.I. must be like these guys in English and American Lit. that only wrote so later they could be assigned in classes, like Thomas Love Peacock.

"Alzo a century is passed since the novel is wrote, it has the portray of the human problems and the lankwage and the subtle of the irony to have keept alive and of very great dzvalue to us in this day."

We certainly did learn a lot from Professor Bielo in Russian class.

After it was over I traded hateful looks with him, sneezed three or four times, and trudged on in to Humanities with Spicer.

In a way, Humanities was twice as bad as Russian. It was harder, but it was at least interesting. Professor Lucretius Finch was the teacher and he was my adviser, the one got me roped into taking the courses that I had. He advised me in September all about the college, and how the only rule at Liberty was to be a gentleman at all times and asked me if that was clear. I said it seemed perfectly straight to me, and he gave me his snaggle-toothed halfwit smile and said that he would certainly enjoy having me in his course if I was that much of a philosopher. He signed me up for it, and for Russian, and I took Creative Writing, because they said everybody got a B in there, and Religion from Chaplain Erb, which was the only required course at Liberty.

I guess I liked Creative Writing the best. Simon Arnold was the nice old simpleton that gave it, tall and lean and dark, with dyed hair that looked like a bottle of ink had been poured out on his head. He was a writer, and in his whole life I heard Simon Arnold had done one novel, one essay, and one poem. He would sit up there in class with a jar of spiced tea on the table in front of him and sip that tepid tea and get lonelier and lonelier listening to all the sorry stories and junk the boys would write, until he couldn't stand it any more and he would lilt out on some wild, wonderful kick and talk; and sometimes we would be sitting there two or three hours later, never knowing the time had gone, he could talk so glorious.

That was the class I liked; and Bo never missed once, he thought Simon Arnold was God Almighty and was in an ecstasy when he took an A off him. I read Bo's story that he wrote and it seemed pretty puny to me: about a kid that took a walk by the ocean and got misty-minded about the sea and the moon and all that, and it never moved anywhere; but Simon Arnold ate it up. I had been trying to write him a story, but it was hard to know what to write about.

But I liked Lucretius Finch, and Humanities, all right, and respected him. He was a long ways from the halfwit that he looked like. He came at you with a cool needle and dug it out of you, so you sweat, going over all the great writings and stuff, until you had strained your brain and come out with something you never knew was in there for you to say.

He didn't call on me. I sat in there and watched him dig that needle in the other boys, sitting smoking his eternal weed. Lucretius Finch's cigarette was magic, like the man's on the TV. It was always there between the fingers of his left hand that he held right up by his face so you didn't know whether he was fixing to smoke the cigarette or investigate his nose. He sat there or paced around, speaking just when he had to and soft and fine, with no particular accent except to be scarcely human talk, at a pitch where it could just be heard. This morning he eased us through young Dante's *Inferno*, and got Bo Duddley to explaining the glory of it, and all the levels of sinners, and Bo read aloud some passages, and this one passage starring two guys Roger and Ugolino and one of them was eating the other's head, and it was really glorious.

We ran from that class and hit the car and finessed old Liberty. We took off driving in the T Bird and Bo and I were so happy we would of shouted, sung, and caroled except for Spicer wedged between suitcases in the back seat, never saying a word, quiet as a Yogi, sitting huge-eyed between the suitcases with his thin legs arranged at angles over my duffle bag and his thin lips zippered and blue with cold: I had the feeling he dreaded going home.

We made good time, and about halfway we came into some snow, but we rammed on through, rolling and coasting up and down high hills covered with ice and snow and zooming on over the next one and zigging through stalled cars. We went non-stop and motored into Cincinnati the next day and Spicer directed me to where he lived in a big old cold house on a hill. Spicer's family's name went back to the first brewery or something, and even though they were busted now of course they were pretty high up there in the social scene. We stayed at his house, and me and Bo had a room together, and Spicer's parents came and told us how did we do and what a thrill it was to have us, and that was about the last we saw of

28

them. Spicer was Bo's second cousin, or maybe it was third.

I bought myself a penguin suit and Bo was pleased with how I looked, and I never mentioned how many times I had squired the duchesses at Fiesta-time.

And Lord, did the champagne and stuff ever flow there at Cincinnati. Hell, it submerged Xmas; and they had all these name bands playing all this sickly-sounding junk and they didn't even start the music till 10 p.m. and then continued on all night, and had orchids in the urinals at the country club, which you got to admit is the height of something, and we cavorted around there in Cincinnati. Most of the boys there forgot that debutantes are just women so I had a pretty good time no-competition-wise.

One big stacked old German girl named Gretchen was there that was supposed to be engaged to Michael Spicer so I was very polite to her and she kept making me get her drinks of scotch while Spicer would do his courtesy dances and she finally asked me to go for a walk with her. We walked out by the pool with no water in it at the country club under a frozen sky, and she led me into a dressing shed out there, and we talked quite a bit, and she was the world's champion talker, and would kiss you and then want to know what effect it had on you or if you had read Proust or some damn thing, and asked me my philosophy on life while my fingers were so numb I couldn't work her strap, and I said I was watched over by the Golden Horny Bird, and she said I was a terribly wicked boy, and made me tell her all my true-life adventures back in Javalina.

But it got to be awful cold, and she was such a talker, so after I managed just a little titty we held hands and walked back in the dance, and she had me go get her a drink, and danced with old Bo Duddley, and talked his ear off.

That was the night that ended up with me on one side of the long bar table trying to tip it over and about eight million waiters in white jackets on the other side pushing back for dear life, as I recall.

But that sort of dancing around gets old too, and Bo and me both got homesick and he went home and so did I, with about a week of vacation left.

My T Bird Baby drove me all the way to Javalina without stopping or eating much, and Mama cried to see me and Daddy says we should have Xmas all over again. They still had the tree up, and Bubba shot a fine wild turkey and Aglaia went in to Javalina and got more presents for everybody, and we ate that sucker and had a wonderful time. Mama read from the Corinthians, like she always had done. Then I wanted to stay at home, but Daddy asked me if I had learned it all yet, and I knew he was right, but God knows, it was hard.

Chapter Five

AFTER Xmas it was pretty much of a hard slug. It got so I took three or four hot showers every day and would lie up in my room trying to read and listen to Hank Williams and Hank Snow the Singing Ranger and my favorite records. Sometimes I would just lie up there and cut classes and not go to eat, then Bo Duddley would get after me so I would take off into Olive Hill or some other town, to a motel or a hotel, and hole up so nobody could find me for a day, and I could be alone. Bo kept asking me that if winter was here, could spring be far behind? and I got to thinking, pretty far.

And, *hizo mucho frío.* I mean, my hair would freeze on my head walking across campus from the gym and the ground was hard as iron under your boots. I ached to go back home. But, I didn't. I stayed right there at Liberty and froze my rear end off and tried to study all that mess and like to went ape. Bo was looking forward to the initiation in April and the others were planning for the Spring Retreat, but old Redwine would of settled for some sun.

One night I went to dinner, in the big dining room of mahagony and stone, and Turk Randy had brought a guest to dinner. Miss Vera.

Bo and I had walked over the campus to the dining hall. The path was stiff and the trees along the edge creaked with cold. You could smell a good wood fire off somewhere. A sliver of moon hung up in the sky.

Bo stopped on the path, looking back at Old Liberty.

"Look at it, Redwine," he said.

I saw it, and the woods beyond, and noticed how really dead the trees seemed, with only a spot of year-round dull green here and there. It looked like snow again, and there was a hammerhead cloud back yonder over Old Liberty.

We went in to eat, and there was Vera. She sat at the head of the Iota table with Randy and the actives and I tried not to notice her. Mrs. P.J. was there too. We had the same old monotonous meal. The whole school ate in there, it was a huge, high room. The boys started songs every fifth bite. A bishop was visiting, and had kept us from the trough for a good while with some mumbledy prayer, patting his fat hands over the slope of his belly. He was sitting at the head table with the president. The president was about as big as a dime and sat all through the meal and smoked cigarettes in a holder and never ate bite one, but just roared with laughter whenever the bishop said anything to him. They called him

Monkey because he had wild hair and wild crackly eyes like a monkey. I kept my eyes on those two, and the boys sang some raunchy songs, but the bishop didn't seem to mind. He was a fat old robed bishop and was busy eating. He ate his own pie, then he ate the president's dessert, then he ate the next pie on down the line.

At last we all stood and sang the school song, it wasn't very inspiring. I saw where I had spilled gravy on my shirt.

Turk Randy and P.J. escorted the ladies out, and I took a walk and then drove out of Liberty, by the gravel road that swung along the side of the campus to the wider, rutty road into Olive Hill. She'd never looked at me. I drove the Baby slowly between the stone pillars at the gates of the college. They were lighted up and one of them had the date when some fine old boy had come out into the woods with an ax and a rifle and a Bible to found Liberty College; and the other said the Truth would make you free, in Latin. I gunned the T Bird, the gravel shot out under her dainty wheels, and we made it into Olive Hill in a minute flat and just barely could stop for the first red light.

I drove through the cold black night out of Olive Hill onto the highway south, and when I came to the big four-lane highway it had begun to snow and sleet. It came down more and more so I turned around and drove like a turtle back to town and to the campus; and the car wheels had to gum through snow and mud, and it took me a long time to get back. I felt pretty worn down then. In the dorm I learned that some of the boys had had a sneak affair with the Whale. Old Bo came down to my room and told me what he'd heard about it, and he was pretty disgusted and I was too. I poured Bo and me a little Jack Black each and we sipped that and talked a while, then he went back down the hall to where Gee was snoring, and I tried to write a letter home but couldn't, and just sat on the bed and looked at the painting of the buffalo charging across a prairie full of dust and sun that I had along one wall, and then turned off the lights and lay quiet trying to go to sleep.

Some sleet slammed down outside. When I woke up in the morning it was all frozen into a tight silver glaze of ice and snow and was still drizzling, and I went back to sleep, and every time I woke up I forced myself back to sleep again, and I spent the next day in the room, listening to the sleet drip down.

Chapter Six

I LOOKED out the tremendous round window of our big lounge room they called the Eye and it seemed we were sitting right in the sky. Snow was on the ground and trees were all cracking with ice and shining under a moon, and I almost felt some foreverness looking out from the very top of Old Liberty, almost like a Texas night. I listened to what the boys were saying, sitting up there late at night, lolling around the room on the rugs or on the deep lovely dark leather window seats. I listened and tried not to let their talk eat on me too bad.

"I feel," Spicer was saying, "that we are presently in abeyance of time, between two great somethings. That we have a little leeway now in our lives, personally, and I guess, that the whole world situation is rather the same. That we are not yet too beset, but are in a safe haven; that we can still contemplate and think of things in terms of the abstract; that we are—you know?—uncommitted to some damn thing we don't really want and don't really understand. It's like—well, it's like, just being here, like this, now, like the very middle of the pendulum swing—or like the big tick of the clock in the library reading room, which comes a second or so before the hand actually moves and we are committed to a change in time—it's an eerie time now, I think—a strange feeling—as if we had a moment to prepare for life—or for what is going to come—if we would—if we knew what in hell to prepare for. But, of course, we don't."

"Bull-frog," I said. "No times are different from any other. It's just who you are when you're there. Just the people are different. Like, my Daddy probably sat up here twenty-five years ago and says something like you said just now."

"No," Bo said. "It's beyond that, Redwine, with us, *now*. I get the feeling we're in a vacuum time too."

I nodded at Bo. I knew I was in one. But I wasn't really with him, or with them.

"Old Socrates Spicer has got a point for once, dad," Rojo said, sprawling up in a window seat. "You got a nice ranch or something to go back to, so maybe you don't feel it so much. Me, what I'm looking forward to? A nice job selling death insurance, an apple-colored Falcon of my very own, a little wife with nice jabongoes to kiss me hello every night, a mess of kids, and two weeks salary at a motel just outside Miami for vacation? I could care less."

"That should not be sneezed at," Harmon Baumberg says, eating oranges and cookies on the rug.

"Sure. Granted," Rojo says. "So those things are important—"

"Especially them jabongoes, hoss."

"But there's something else, I hope. I mean, life ain't dedi-

34

cated only to the wife and kids and the power-edger, is it? Like, who was it went home and put a bullet through his head? Then one time, after you have fussed at the kids, and gave the little woman hell for burning the veal cutlets, you're sitting out on the front porch wishing you could get yourself a new Buick like old Jones' across the street and you look up, and it's all nice and twilight, and you see this beautiful huge damn mushroom cloud gliding across the sky toward you, and what do you do then?"

"You say, consider the mushroom cloud, how lovely it is, how incredibly lovely and true," says old Cristóbal Gottlieb, a fag from Argentina.

"I'd get down on my knees and pray to God Almighty," I said.

"Try that now—not just Redwine—and maybe we won't have to look up there and see it," says Little Dick. "Or maybe that would be God up there."

"Wouldn't that be terrible?" Bo said, in a little while. "Just watching that thing and then waiting to die from the radiation? God!"

"No funnier than being an old person—sixty-five or seventy or eighty—and knowing that death is sure to come in a year or two, or a minute," Spicer said, puffing on that silly sophomore's pipe of his out in the middle of the floor. "I wish sometimes, here, that I had something like the nearness of death—to intensify life."

I snorted. Spicer wanted to intensify life. Some little guy snuggled over by me on the window seat and turned his milky eyes on me and whispered, "You got to dig life deep, man, like, when you're living. Friends, man, and loyalty, that's the only true kick."

It was the best thing that had been said, but he started to snuggle in closer, and I saw who he came with, Señor Cristó-

35

bal Gottlieb, and I leaned over and whispered to him if he got near me I would break his ass. That bugged me so horribly, I didn't see how a boy could be a fag.

"Still it's a wonderful time," Bo was saying, "being here, with so many new ideas and philosophies and challenges coming at you, and you're groping among them, unsure, except basically, of what to believe or really just what your ideas are. I know I am. It's a hard time of life all the way around, I guess, but it's important, and interesting. But not nearly as great as I thought it was going to be. I always try to live for each day, but it's hard in the college routine where you plan for your next class and keep telling yourself you'll really *do* something later. You spend all your time either wishing time would go by in a hurry or slowly. I wonder what you think in regard to these days that sped by with nothing to mark them and meant nothing but another day to you when you get old and, like Michael says, are sure of dying soon. I wish you *didn't* have to search so long and through so much, and let so much time go by in searching before you get to life. Because I know it's true, the Indian poem, that this day is life, the very life of life. All the verities and realities *are* there. But which are they?"

I looked out at the snow on the ground and the ice on the trees.

"I had in mind, to begin with, something more specific and less mawkish," Spicer says, trying to load the shiny pipe and dribbling tobacco over his crossed legs. "I had in mind the specific situation of being not just *in* the sixties—or the thirties—or 4 B.C.—or 1984—but *now,* and all this specific time-context means. It makes a difference. Things are of this minute, there'll be new bases for things the next minute. My God, we're in a whole new era. That's what I meant. I don't know if we can learn anything here that isn't obsolete already —for the coming situation. Maybe we're obsolete. Just think

36

—man is getting free, really completely free, for the first time. He won't be earth-bound, or word-bound, maybe not even time-bound—that's what I wonder and don't understand."

"Yeah," some Womb guy says, "how is any of this crud we study relevant?"

"An encouraging kick," Rojo says.

"I have to disagree," Bo said then. "What are you studying? Literature, history, languages, math, religion, philosophy? It can't all get obsolete."

"Why not, man?"

Harmon Baumberg spit out a mouthful of orange seeds. "You don't think it's relevant, death? How to face it, what it is? Who is God? What you can do, caught in the web? You think you get anywhere, going to the moon? Spicer? You think you are going to get out of life? What do you think the Bible's about, just not to fornicate, and stay away from your neighbor's ass, and be a boy scout? It answers, what is God? And all the questions."

"Like philosophy tries to do, and literature," Bo says.

"I would as soon talk to a group of mental patients," Spicer says, making like he is real disgusted because everybody hasn't just rolled over and kicked up their legs in ecstasy over his ideas. "You don't comprehend. You will, though"—and he sneered around at all of us "—you certainly will. Just wait until that pendulum swings over into the future—five years? —ten years? Come see me in ten years and see if anything we've said here or done up till now, until this minute, or thought was the truest and most eternal and certain thing in the world makes any difference then. Or maybe twenty years. It's like the future world had slipped in on us in the dark and got us about three months pregnant, just enough so we know that we are, but we don't have any idea of what we're going to bring forth."

"Better watch that old rape complex there, Spicerino," Rojo says.

"The baby will come forth either black or yellow, and you will never find him in Old Liberty," Gottlieb says.

"That's nice talk," says Little Dick. "In fact," Dick says, "this is all so swell-sounding that I think I'll go down to the chapel and sit there and let it all dissolve and go back in the void where it belongs. That baby won't be black or yellow or any one thing. Things won't be much different for it. Twenty years? Get serious, men. We might try that atomic reaction that got started once, but somehow got stopped by talk and screwing around just like this here."

"Yes?" Spicer said.

"Love, man. Love."

Spicer didn't say much to that, he wasn't very big on love.

"Where in the Bible does it say that about not fornicating?" I said. "I never saw that."

I quit looking out the window and got up and grabbed one of Baumberg's oranges. There were some philosophical points I would of liked to know about, on sex.

"It's there," Harmon said. "And the orange you're welcome to, but the seeds I don't need back."

"I never knew it came right out and forbid that, as a commandment," I said.

"It's the one Harmon mentioned about thy neighbor's ass," Rojo said.

"Wise guy," I said, standing up there in the Eye with all of them looking at me. "I don't know," I said. "There's a hell of a lot to this. Can't you guys ever talk about real things, for God's sake? This is the damn 'life of life' too. I mean, I know there's a moral law, and all. But, *a veces,* in different situations, for different people—well, it's an awfully human thing to do, ain't it?"

"You are the great expert," Spicer says.

"Ask the old horn-horn bird," Rojo says.

I threw the orange at him.

"It's just wrong," Bo says.

"I'll show you in the Bible," Little Dick says, as if he would really like to.

"Sure it's human," Baumberg says. "What else is so human? So they tell me. Who gets a chance in this hole? Wrong? Right? A law is a law, Redwine."

"It's fine, if you're an animal in rut," Spicer says, "but not so fine and human if you're a real person, with enough moral fiber and intellectual strength not to worry about those situations, or need them. Thoreau said there were times when he felt he could seize a woodchuck and devour it raw, but that wasn't when he considered himself most a human being."

"This ain't about woodchuck, Spicer, and no real man says pooh-pooh, toodledeedee, and doesn't consider all this, it's pretty damned important. Only an idiot never gets horny and hears the Cry. And it goes beyond that, with some, I guess—not me, you smirking bunch of eunuchs. Are you guys being honest? I'd like to know.

"I mean, say you have the chance with this hide—like, say the Whale, or somebody that doesn't care, like her—and you don't. Why not, really? Are you held back by some invisible hand, or what? How come *she's* not held back by the same invisible hand? Or, if you do? Is it right because *she* wants you to? What is it keeps you back or drives you on, or is driving her to be a hide? This is what I'm asking you holy devils —can there be such a commandment, from God, Who's supposed to understand—how can it always fit—I mean, man is a strange animal. . . ."

"Walker," Spicer said, "your ramblings have all the force and effectiveness of *merde* thrown wildly through an iron gate."

"Spicer," I told him, "if you want to say 'crap' say 'crap.'"

But they just ragged me on it, and thought I was only trying to find an excuse for being the horniest one at Liberty. Or else they were afraid to talk out plain about it with Spicer there, because he was such a superior sneering sophomore.

"It's just not right," Bo said, walking back down. "Morality isn't what *you* feel like doing, Redwine. Or you and some other person. That's what always gets me about when you come in after some conquest with one of those cigars you smoke, wondering if you haven't hurt some real nice girl."

"There are all kinds of girls, Bo," I said. "That's part of what I'm getting at, I guess, whether some of them are worth the cigar."

In my room it kept swarming around in my mind. There really were things that wouldn't come straight for me. There was no need Spicer being so holier than anybody, and I thought I would see if he was a real philosopher and would talk some more, or maybe I just wanted to ask him how he could be so frozen up and be in the same world as me. So I went over in the Womb where he lived. When I got there and went in his room I eased on back out quick, leaving Spicer in that room full of books all by himself. I should of knocked, but was glad I didn't. I always felt sorry for him, after that, the poor fool and his philosophy.

Chapter Seven

I HAVEN'T done a very good job of showing you the whole picture of the college, but if you ever come across the yearbook of Liberty College, the *Libertarian*, for this year, you can get a good idea of the scene.

Right at the front is a photo of Monkey, the president, and then next to him old Dean Prigge, that nobody ever saw after the first day except at meals, and he stayed in the basement section of Old Liberty where he had a room down at one end of a deserted hall. He was pretty old, but he used to make it to those meals all right. Monkey and Dean Prigge, and of course the faculty, were all the administration Liberty had, but for Miss Pigeon. She is pictured in her little cap, the nurse that kept the infirmary next to the dining hall, which was right convenient at that.

Next is a photo of old Gilly, and underneath it calls him Custodian of Buildings and Grounds. He was the chief janitor in Old Liberty, and he would sweep, or mop, or clean the johnnies in there every once in a while, but he didn't pay much attention to the rest of the buildings, except for the chapel, which was kept up nice, and they had some other old boys that cleaned up too. Old Gilly was a wonderful man. He had white hair and blue Irish eyes and always a scraggly beard and stumped through the halls of Old Liberty about 5 a.m. every Sunday morning, scrounging anything, whisky, gin, or beer, that happened to be left from the parties the night before. Gilly had a false leg, on at the hip, and Spicer used to say he bet it was made of ivory; but I knew Gilly wasn't that well off, to have an ivory leg; and he was the happiest man I ever saw, except for my Uncle Sweet, who has never been off the ranch.

Then right next to Gilly in the yearbook is a photo of Chaplain Erb. He ran the chapel at the college. Liberty wasn't denominational, and the services generally were just high Protestant. It was a beautiful chapel.

Then there are pictures of all the seniors individually, and there are 54 of them. Then photos of the juniors and of the sophomores and then the freshmen; there were 392 students at Liberty College total. I slept through it when they made the freshman group picture so you won't see me in that one but you can find Bo there, the little guy with glasses on in the back row, the third from the left at the end of the line that is standing on the dorm steps.

You can see most of the guys I have been telling about in these photos, and Spicer is right in the middle of the sophomore group; and Turk Randy, and Smoke Smith, and P.J. all have photos in with the seniors, and Horsehead does too, he was a senior and supposed to graduate. You can't miss him, a poor pitiful creature that couldn't talk in words and would make you sick to look at him but wasn't really stupid or an idiot like you would think.

Next in the book come all the teachers in the various departments. A bunch of birds in Chemistry and Physics and so on that I never did know, except to see them hotfooting between labs and classes and meals. Simple Sampson of History, and in his picture he looks very distinguished but like a mummy they had imported from Egypt and wedged behind a desk so that he would crumble if you touched him, and who would ever suspect he would be the one of the faculty to bang on that rinky-tink and shout out about that Indian maid? Then young Libido Al of Psychology and Adam Marks of Eco. They would take off every weekend and go to Pittsburgh where they had a pad and try to seduce all the girls that would come in from the colleges around. And there were some more. Professor Lucretius Finch, of course, looking like an absolute halfwit; and Simon Arnold, he is the handsomest one in the whole yearbook, only he looks lonelier than ever without the jar of tea set there before him; and Milo Martin, that was in the English department too, only I never got to know him but Bo said he was all right and liked him. And Chaplain Erb taught Religion; and his picture is in there a third time, because he was the sponsor of the drama club that was going to do *A Midsummer Night's Dream* and I was going to be Bottom and old Slugger was going to be Oberon King of the Fairies and Cristóbal Gottlieb was going to be his queen Titania, and don't you know they would of had a time at that?

It was a pretty brilliant and distinguished faculty, and we were really proud of them. It seemed like half the books in the library one or another of them had done it, and if some of them weren't worth a wrinkled prune as teachers, I guess you can't expect too much.

All the fraternities have photos then, and a bunch of the inhabitants of the Womb in a big lump photograph. You can find Redwine Walker in the Iota bunch standing up in the back row, and the one with a fancy vest is Smoke Smith again; all the guys are there, and Bo is sitting cross-legged in front of the group, with Rojo, and Bo looks kind of scared in that picture.

But the best pictures of all are the various ones they had left over down in the *Libertarian* office and threw in the back of the yearbook. There's one of me and Bo wrestling around in the snow outside the dorm I wouldn't take a golden buck for, and there're pictures of various parties on Low Floor and on Top Floor and even a pathetic thing or two of them trying to live it up in the Womb. There're pictures of guys partying obviously bombed, and there's one priceless shot of a bunch at Dutch's—the guy in the middle leaning over so that the camera could center on him is Monroe Gee and if you ever look this one up, don't be shocked, because he is giving his little gesture to whom it may concern. That is the only appearance of Monroe Gee in the yearbook. There are a mess of others: there's the photo Rojo took of Harmon Baumberg sitting there in his room crying on his birthday after he had got a big hairy chocolate cake from his mama and we found out and everybody went in there and helped themselves to big gougy handfuls of it. It was good cake, but then we were sorry, right after, that Harmon didn't get any. Another picture is of Vera and Mrs. P.J. and P.J. and Turk Randy and Smoke Smith standing in the den, and Mrs. P.J. looks pretty clobbered, and Randy and Smoke Smith are on either side of Vera (she is the Oriental-looking girl) and Randy has his arm around her waist.

I almost forgot, there is a big picture of Old Liberty hunched up over two pages in the exact center of the book, and of course you would want to see that, with the huge windows of the Eyes on the towers, and Bo's room the corner one on the fourth floor on the north side, i.e. the right side of the photo as you look at it. The towers on Old Liberty go right off the page.

You couldn't buy my *Libertarian* for a billion or two dollars, it is one of the dearest things I have. I hope you get the chance to see one, sometime.

Chapter Eight

FEBRUARY was a long month.

It snowed again, then it came a blizzard, and you couldn't even get out of there driving, and we were locked up in the cold bosom of Old Liberty. It was cold as hell then; the radiator would screech and bang but not much heat came up. It melted, with a couple of halfway decent days; only to have the rain start, an endless hard cold rain, until you were soggy and cold through to your soul; Mama shipped me more blankets, and the Mexican food she sent kept me alive. We would go pick it up, and then Bo and Rojo and me would have a feast of hot enchiladas and tostadas and pepper sauce and Mexican beer I kept a case of in my room.

Whenever the rain stopped for a minute, it would freeze. And I stayed in bed and shivered and hated the Goddamn Yankee country bad as I had to begin with all over again; and I spent a night in a nice warm motel in Olive Hill with a girl that didn't have such a particularly gorgeous face, in fact she was ugly, but kind of plump and soft; and after the Horny Bird flew away for a while I was tired and pleasant-feeling enough to come back—smoking me a Kopar, to let them know that Redwine wasn't slipping and hadn't just been idle.

Bo had stopped studying and reading quite as much and had got depressed. I tried to talk him into taking off on a trip to Mexico with me, but he wouldn't do it. We spent a lot of time together then, in February and March, while Liberty was heading for the Spring Retreat at the beginning of April. Rojo was initiated into Iota just before the Retreat; and we were supposed to become members of the sacred order at the end of April. Every Monday night was the Mickey Mouse time, when the fraternity had its meetings, in the secret room in the Iota suite. One Monday Smoke Smith got upset about how spastic it was all getting to be, and said he knew the Bull up there was getting pretty displeased at our attitude, and then all the actives griped and threatened about what a disgraceful-appearing group of pledges they had. So they told us we all had to wear the gray suits and Liberty ties, even me, to all the meetings. The next Monday we revolted. They about depledged us, they were mad as a hornet, but laughing too.

I wore some filthy chinos and my old taped-up moccasins and a yellow candy-striped cowboy shirt with pearl buttons. Old Bo wore bright blue britches and a dark blue work shirt and a green and white tie, tied in a huge Windsor knot with Harmon Baumberg's horse-tweed coat. Rojo had on especially green corduroy britches, a waiter's coat, and some eighth-grade tie. The other pledges did the same. We went over pretty big. Then we bent over low, while Turk Randy and Slugger had a fine game of tennis using us as balls; we had to go jump over a chair and turn back around and bend down and hold our ankles while they whopped us with big paddles with the Iota crest on them. I didn't take to that; it was the first time they had done more than a tap or two. Randy was a little loaded and kept going to the pony keg in the den and then come back to play the game.

Pretty soon I saw that Bo was lying on the floor where the Randy ape had cracked him with the paddle, and Turk Randy was yelling for him to get up and run and jump over the chair; but I could see that Bo was trying pretty hard not to cry. Randy had hit on the tailbone.

"Better let it alone, Turk," I said.

Bo got up, it nearly killed him. "I can take it," he says.

"You don't need to take it from anybody that's a little gone," I said.

"Huh?" Smoke Smith said. "Listen, Redwine. Listen here. Boy? You better watch yourself. Hey, get in this line-up here—pledge line-up here, all you men—yeah—stand at attention. Redwine, suck it in. Huh? Better apologize to Mr. Randy, 'fore he gets mad. Better do. Ain't that right, Redwine?"

Turk Randy came over to the line-up breathing beer, and he was a big one. He wore this beautiful letter sweater of Liberty blue with a big gold L on it. He was captain of the football team, and it had been the first team in the history of Liberty to be undefeated all season. He was a tackle and he stood there, and was bigger than most of the pledges put together.

"Walker," he says, "I have tried to be patient with you, mostly because you are a legacy and I thought I would make the best of the bad bargain Iota got with you—but I've had it now, up to here, with your damn arrogance and sticking your chest out and carrying on around here like you were the initiate and we were all your little servants, or something. You hear me?"

I could of hit him and if he'd called me a son of a bitch or anything I would of, of course. But all I could think was Bo was all right now, and how glad Daddy was when I joined Iota. So I just stood there stony-eyed while he abused me a good bit more.

"You know what a pledge is lower than, Walker?"

"No, sir."

47

"Duddley?"

"Whalecrap on the bottom of the ocean, sir."

"Walker—so what are you lower than?"

"I got no idea," I says.

"Look, Walker," he says, right in my face. "I would as leave depledge you as tear the wings off a fly that was bothering me. Now let's try again. You know, Red-water, this isn't just a social club—it's got advantages a hell of a long ways beyond that—which you, with your little immature mind, can't even imagine yet. If we have to refine you guys' spirits with the paddle and not always be just your buddies and your playmates, well, hell, we're sorry. But we got to get you ready. Don't you realize you're supposed to be *initiated*—into all the full benefits of Iota—in a couple months, Walker? Personally, I doubt you ever make it. All you know or appreciate about fraternity could be written on the wrapper of one of those damn cigars." By this time he was jabbing his finger on my chest and I stood there at attention, making my eyes look dead like a wetback's do when Daddy is giving him hell. "This isn't just a frolic or an excuse for you to come to our parties—this is *brotherhood!*

"Now," he says again, stepping back, "let us see. What is a pledge lower than, Walker?"

"Whalecrap, sir, on the bottom of the ocean."

"Sure. Now—you are a pledge. Right? So, what does that make you, Walker?"

I stared at him.

"It makes him a damn fool for standing there listening to you," P.J. says. "Lay off, sport. Let's get this meeting underway. I got to get to the house, or my old lady'll be burned. Every time I'm late she thinks the Whale's been here."

"Usually has. Huh?" says Smoke Smith, everybody laughs, that snaps it. We have separate meetings—Bo is the leader of the pledge class—and then we come back together and fill

48

the glasses and mugs and everybody ends up by singing the fraternity songs and marching around the suite.

Afterwards the big ape tracked me down again. He was mad. He caught me when he still had a pretty good audience.

"Don't let him bug you," Rojo whispered. "He's just one guy."

Bo looked at me and him. He knew my feelings, he was a legacy too.

"Okay, big dog," Turk says. "I want to show you something. I'm not a member now, and you're not a pledge, see? Just two guys. You think you're a big man, you can call me down in meeting. Okay. Let's see if you are. Wrestle, box, just slug it out—what do you want, big dog?"

"You got fifty pounds on him," Bo said.

"That's all right," I said. "Except, I ain't mad at you, Turk. I don't want to fool with you, box or wrestle or nothing."

"Oh, come *on*," he says.

"Tell you what," I said. "You want to Indian wrestle? Not the arm on the table, but stand-up? Since you have to."

We did. We stood foot to foot and locked hands and he like to broke mine, he was strong, and I almost pulled him off the mark right at first with a quick twist down; but then he started to yanking and wrenching and he was too heavy; so soon he gave a big effort and I went flying onto the rug. Then he was satisfied; he had showed me up; and I suppose some of them thought I was chicken not to have fought him, but that would of been it. Bo blamed himself for the whole thing. I was glad it worked out I didn't have to fight Turk Randy for real, because it wouldn't of been any box or wrestle or just whatnot then.

"You two be best of friends," Smoke Smith said, clapping me on the back. "Best friends. Respect each other now. Old Turk fine fella. Yeah? You know he really likes old Redwine —told me. Sure. Did."

"Don't let the big clown bother you," P.J. told me. "It's the rain and ice, and this damn dorm. He's got to pick on somebody. Say, when can you come over and have dinner with me and Janie and the kids? How about that? Sure. Good. No strain, boy. Stay loose, Redwine."

P.J. was an old bald toad that talked like ten years ago but it made me feel better.

I read nine million books that month, some required but some just because I wanted to.

One time when we were shooting the bull, Spicer, who liked to pick out certain subjects and then make everybody talk about it, brought up books: what was your favorite book and who was your favorite author? I said A. Conan Doyle was mine, and next I guessed James Fenimore Cooper, that wrote *The Last of the Mohicans* about Uncas and his daddy Chingachgook and Le Renard Subtil, he was the Indian against them. That old man in that book. He reminded me of Uncle Sweet, the way he could shoot, though he surely did talk put-on. But A. Conan Doyle was the best.

"I never figure you for a Sherlock Holmes fan," Bo said.

"No, not that. Not all that Watson mess. I mean, *The White Company* and about Sir Nigel Loring, and all like that."

"You're kidding," Spicer said.

But that reminded me of those books, and I went to the library, way back up in the stacks. *The Last of the Mohicans* was there, and *The White Company* too, in there with all the Pope and Milton and Wordsworth and those birds. It was like seeing an old friend, reading those books again. Then I looked for *The Little Shepherd of Kingdom Come,* which I had liked, but they didn't keep it in the library.

My literary views weren't very close to Bo's or Spicer's or

anybody else's that met up in the Eye, even on things we all were reading together. Simon Arnold gave us a pack of books to read. You had to read several and write a paper on them to pass the course. I read *The Way of All Flesh* because Simon Arnold loved it, but it was the hardest book I ever tried to get into.

We all read *The Return of the Native*, only he wasn't a real native at all, but a poor slob named Clem that I could never seem to get with. We talked this book over a couple of times and Bo let me see his paper that he pulled an A on. Bo's paper said that old Hardy loaded the dice against Clem and Eustacia, the beautiful gal in the book, and that it was the Heath, the environment, was the thing holding them all down so. I could see all that, I guess, but God Almighty, I couldn't swallow it. Bo Duddley wrote what a noble old boy Clem was, and how sensitive and strung-up Eustacia was on account of being all hunkered down on the Heath; but I couldn't buy it. I wrote that Clem was an idiot to come back there if he wasn't going to do something active about licking that Goddamn Heath, and how Eustacia seemed a weak sister to me. I wrote that you were a damn fool if you sat around and let anybody load the dice on you. I didn't get any A, so I guess Bo had it right. Rojo said not to worry, though, that *The Return of the Native* was strictly nowhere as a book nowadays anyway. I guess I enjoyed reading it even better than Bo did, especially that reddleman, Diggory, and I was sure glad to see him get fixed up with that other little gal at the end. They were at least human beings.

In the Eye, Spicer led a discussion on who was your favorite painter, then your favorite poet, without Redwine; but I went up there in the philosopher discussion and said Aristippus because Bo wanted me to so bad, and everybody did get tickled; but I couldn't defend it very well; I had been knowing pleasure wasn't the highest for a long time before Mr. Lucretius Finch said so, no matter what those old boys thought.

Sunday we went to church in the chapel. Chaplain Erb put on the service, in his gown and getup. Bo and I sat and prayed in a long cool wooden carved row as the organ played gorgeous music.

I went to take Communion with the line of kneelers at the altar. Horsehead and Little Dick knelt on one side of me, and Bo on the other, and it was peaceful, kneeling at the altar in the chapel.

I went off into a long reverie before the chaplain passed on to me with the Body and the Blood. I thought of Bo, and of Horsehead and Dick next to me, and of something I had read one day leafing through Bo's journal that he kept, a passage that said:

L.D. & Hhead: *The person who is left out and neglected by the majority, and then receives decent treatment from someone he likes, has been given a channel to life by that person. How dare we not? I am Hhead.*

After, I said, "Come on, Bo, and go to church with me now."

"Is that what you do after chapel? Go to church again? We wondered where you sneaked off to."

We drove along a frozen side road of Olive Hill and turned off into the woods.

"What are they hiding back here? Voodoo?"

"Not hardly."

We went to the Liberty Baptist-Methodist. It was far enough back in the woods not to be noticed, but near the college and the town still. We hit the 11 o'clock service. It was a Baptist service one week and Methodist the next. This week it was Methodist. The preacher was Baptist all the time.

We sang and there was a fine old lady behind me that would of put a screech-owl to shame, and an old man next to Bo Duddley that between hacking and spitting in the aisle had some trouble managing the tunes. It was a wooden church, painted white inside and out, and there was a little platform with a stand for the preacher to lean on at the front. The congregation was the choir; there wasn't any organ. It was fun to stand up on your hind legs and sing those good old songs.

They had the Creed and the long preacher's prayer and the giving and then the preacher commenced on the sermon. Cowlicks sprouted at all angles from the top of his head. I always had a secret laugh, wondering if the preacher wasn't Monkey's brother, he had the same wild hair and eyes. He had a hard twang to his voice that set you on edge and made you follow every word he preached.

The preacher spoke of the sins of the people against a God that in His loving-kindness had sent His only Son to save them. Salvation was promised to them that would receive their Savior, but them that rejected him were lost. Worst were the hypocrites that professed to accept Him and yet in their hearts did not.

"Think, my friends," the preacher said, "think of this. Jesus Christ, your Lord Jesus Christ, the only begotten Son of God, was brought before Pontius Pilate in Je-rusalem. They brought before him also Barabbas the murderer, and one of them was to go free. And Pontius Pilate addressed the throng of people and he cried unto them, 'Which of these men shall I set free? Here is Barabbas, who is a murderer and a thief and the scum of the earth, and here is this man Jesus, that seems to be a good man and has done no evil that I can see. Which of them shall I set free?' And they replied, shouting—oh, can you imagine it my brothers and sisters?—they shouted, 'Free Barabbas!' 'Free Barabbas!' was what they shouted.

"They had then your Lord, your own Jesus, and they said 'Free the murderer Barabbas!' They rejected their Savior! And Pontius Pilate asked unto them, so what am I going to do with this man Jesus? They replied, oh the shame of it, they answered, 'Crucify him!'

" 'Cruci-fy him,' they yelled and they took the Lamb of God out unto the mountain of Calvary and they butchered Him! Can you see, can you see? They rejected their Lord.

"Now—beware you too do not reject your Lord. For He is always near you, seeking entrance into your hearts. It is as if He were standing by your back door, standing out by your door in the rain and the ice on a cold bitter day like this, and you go and lock the door. Each time you lock your soul against Christ you reject Him as did those before you. And each time you reject Him you re-cruci-fy Him!"

Then the preacher asked for souls that would accept salvation to hurry down the aisle, and we sang.

We sang, "Were You There When They Crucified My Lord?" that lady and that man near us, and all of us, Bo was singing too.

A couple of folks went down there, a good old farmer and a big girl. In a while the girl turned around and showed us her ugly face and started telling us all how glad she was to get salvation and how rotten she'd been, and she kept at it for quite a while, kind of like this:

"I was a slave to sin that cherished every kind of deception and evil. Oh, I lied, backbit, envied, hated, I was full of haughtiness, greed, deceit, and selfishness. I did every kind of evil and I enjoyed doing it. I could not honestly accept the fact of my own wickedness. Oh thank God that He has provided for my desperate situation! God in His infinite mercy

54

has joined me with Someone as different from me as bliss from despair. The One I am now uniting with is perfect love, purity, and strength. He is clean and I am filth and yet He seeks me for His own. He has reached out for me here today where I lay groveling in the muck of existence. He has promised me rest in Him."

She went on a good bit beyond that. She was a schoolteacher and she could toss the words around. It sure made the preacher happy.

"It seemed like she was looking right at you all the time she was shouting up there," Bo said, driving back to Liberty.

"Sure enough?" I said.

She was the old girl I had shacked up with in town. I hoped she wasn't pregnant.

"We take some swell courses," Rojo said.

"Sometimes I'd like to make the professors go to hear each other's lectures, and see if *they* know what they're polluting the breeze about," somebody said.

"It sure does help when they can't even talk English," I said. "Like yesterday, in Russian, here's old Professor Bielo sucking his black teeth and obviously not thinking about the perfective tense he was supposed to be reviewing us on, but about you know who. So he really fixes me up for learning that stuff. 'Some imperfectives can form back perfectives by expending their stems,' he says. 'Fine,' I say. Then he grins around very happy, like he's made a big point that has been troubling him for a number of years and chuckles out with, 'The students get very quickly across the idea.' Sure we do. Then he goes back to it: 'Just esk yourself when dealing with perfectives: did I get it over with?' 'Okay,' I say, 'I will.' Pretty soon he is in orbit again over some old hack of a Russky textbook writer, and telling us about his style, and he ends up the period in a blaze of Bielo with 'In

55

lankwage I do not like pretensions like saying *I transpire* instead of *I sweat!*'"

"Suppose how Mrs. Bielo feels about that?"

"I believe the mumblers are the worst," Rojo says. "I have got this prof in Classics that is an old rubbery chap that comes in and sits down at his table and dredges out these old yellow notes and for a long time he just reads from them with his big flabby lips. You can hear his lips flapping together but you can't distinguish the words. He reads on and on, and if the note cards get mixed up, he just keeps reading. Then he brings out an old beat-up copy of Caesar and we plunge into the translation. Except he sits up there and does all the translating, and you can't hear a diphthong. The only time you hear him is at the bell. Then he looks up and gets real animated and says there will be a test tomorrow over everything we have had today. It's exactly like," Rojo said, "when they inducted me into the Army and the man made me raise up my hand and then said to me 'Mumble, mumble, mumble, and the penalty is death.'"

"You wouldn't figure Physics for a funny course, but it was last week." Bo had come to the party. "The physics professor, you know, old Cyrano, was lecturing and at the end of the class decided to show the assembled students how color affected the refraction of light. So he goes over and turns off the lights, and the automatic shades come down, and a hush falls as he says, 'I will shine this white light on that far wall.' No one could find the white light. 'Now I shall change its color and it will become smaller. Observe.' Now we saw a huge ball of red light. 'Dammit, give me that convex lens.' He drops it. 'Harrumphadamn—give me that other one—' Everybody laughing. 'Now notice that reflection.' We looked and saw his huge banana nose outlined in the red light and looking ever so impressive. We roared. He

56

roared. He'll get some good descriptions of that experiment."

Rojo opened a brew we had let set outside on the window ledge so all the incidental part would freeze and the alcohol could be drained off the top. "That's the way it goes, good buddies," he says, "here today, here tomorrow."

Harmon Baumberg was one of the first ones in the country to have a working pay-TV system. He had a TV set in his room, a 21-inch screen, and you had to pay Harmon $1 to watch it. It was the only one on Top Floor could pull in a picture clearly. Sometimes Harmon had 20 guys crowded up in that dark room, watching the trash. I only went in occasionally to see "Gunsmoke" or "Rawhide" and I liked the pro ball, and they had some pretty good late, late movies, Nazi and horror and old Duke Wayne and Humphrey Bogart movies. I saw *Rio Grande* a number of times.

The thing about it was the commercials. Now it was a hard thing to go to Lucretius Finch's class where it was logic and the really honest conclusions you had to show, and then go into Harmon Baumberg's room and have to see those damn illogical, stupid commercials that acted like you were a nut. And you couldn't get up and leave and come back after the commercial. You paid Harmon $1 every time you came in the room, even if you just went to the head.

This old boy sat on the screen, like he wasn't expecting a soul in the world to visit him. The narrator said, "Aha, I see you are working on a rocket to the moon. What do you big scientists think of our chances to get to the moon soon?" "Oh, no," he says, looking up with a dung-eating grin, "I am no great scientist. I am just the lowly man that sweeps out the elephant stalls at the zoo. I put these rockets together in my spare time for fun." Then the narrator like to had an orgasm. "Ooo," he says, "here is a man that thinks for himself. Yes, sir. And," he says, sly, pretending to be casual and just interested in passing, "what is that you have been clouding up the screen puffing on? The brand?"

"Oh, it's so-and-so," he says.

The narrator asks does he recommend it for everybody.

"Oh, no," he says, "only for those that have got any *sense*."

They had all kinds of swell commercials. They had the achy head with *compartments* to it, and Lord, statues that were so mature they needed deodorant rolled on them. There were a thousand of them you had to wade through to get to John Wayne. I remember this one where this pretty young woman was holding up a thing of tissue and telling you what a wonderful difference there was in it, so you would know right away, and how soft and fine and glorious it was, until you took to thinking it was something elegant you should get your loved one for a gift, and forgot it was toilet paper.

Some nights I would pay old Harmon $7 or $8 to miss the commercials.

The Red Lattice was a townie place, they didn't like Liberty boys. We arrived there, me and Rojo and Bo Duddley. I made them go; she never came to Dutch's.

We pushed in. The Red Lattice was packed. It divided into two rooms—a big one with a long bar and stools and booths with bright, fuzzy lights over them, and a side room. We went in there. A little semicircular bar and nice, dim blue lights and "Red Sails in the Sunset" playing. Four million people crowded in there back to butt. Not a stall empty. I look around.

Some waitress that has got scabies on her face comes charging at us. "What's that?" she screams at Rojo's guitar.

"If it was up your ass you'd know," Rojo says.

"I'll take care of it, ma'am," Bo says.

The bartender called and she got off our back. We were

so sardined in you couldn't scratch and be sure it was you. Townies. Rojo tried to shove to the bar, but he might just as well attempted a little swim in a commode.

I lost sight of Bo. Then I saw him over by a booth where a real big guy and a little guy were sitting with two dollies. I eased over.

Bo has no conception of things, he is trying to be nice. "Redwine," he says, "this is Molly here, and this is Marcy Lou Johnson. I met Marcy Lou at the skating rink a couple weeks ago. I didn't catch these guys' names."

"Shove, four-eyes," the big one says to Bo. Marcy Lou is sweet-looking and young, but you should see Molly's risers. They were fine.

The little guy got up and stuck his finger in Bo's chest. "If I was you, man," he says, "I would collect the Lone Ranger here and get outta here. You are annoying Duke. Most times Duke is very nice but sometimes he gets terrible headaches and has a few beers and can be very mean."

"Duke doesn't look like the headache type to me," Bo says. "What's the matter with him? Migraine?"

The little guy shoved Bo. "Watch what you call Duke," he said.

Rojo came up. "Horse-manure on Duke," he says. "Who is Duke?"

"This jock here," I say.

"Jesus," Rojo says.

"We are leaving," I tell the little guy, only just then I hear the Cry. I leaned over without really being able to help it and pinched old Molly. Up leaped the Duke. Rojo cracks him with the guitar. The place becomes aware. "Get them Liberty mothers," somebody yells. Bo Duddley danced around with Duke's little chum-buddy. We knocked that one down and raged around and made it out the side door, me, Rojo, and dragging Bo.

We ran to the car, we took off in flat nothing. They never saw our vapor.

On a deserted road we stopped and climbed out to take a leak. I pulled a jug from under the seat, and we made a picture, on the snow, sucking at the bottle and letting the road have it. Bo's britches were about torn off.

"You shouldn't've hit Duke," I told Rojo. "He gets headaches."

"Were they real?" he says.

"What, man?"

"You know what, you bastard."

"I don't feel any too sorry for Duke," I said, "where he can put his head when it aches."

"A pleasant evening's diversion," Rojo said. We crawled along home with all the windows down and the night all around us cold and clear.

"Great," Bo said. "I don't know what makes you get those wild notions, Redwine. They were nice girls."

"Very pleasant," I said. "Good clean American-boy fun. Indeedy."

Only, where was Vera?

"Sure, there are times like that," Little Dick said. "Probably the worst was at graduation last year."

Dick was talking. Sometimes I went in there to let Little Dick cool me down. I got so I didn't mind Horsehead, and I would take him things, like my big silver-studded saddle, to admire, and he would grin at me. I don't want to discuss Horsehead; but I got so I didn't mind being in the room with him.

I asked Little Dick if he didn't feel funny about being colored, and resent the fact, when he was so near white, and if it wasn't a pretty big cross to drag.

"At graduation the principal had been speaking for a long

60

time, and then hesitated for a minute," Dick said. "Then he said my name. Redwine, it sounded good. Spoken so importantly and dramatically by the principal. Pride and real elation filled me. And the principal stood impressively on the platform of the school auditorium, waiting to shake my hand and give me the book, wrapped in white with a blue ribbon, that he held.

"A book. Well, Redwine, I laughed. The prize was a book. I thought I had probably read it three times already. So I rose up out of the mass of seniors self-consciously. So many thoughts came to me at once, and the unimportant and silly thoughts crowded my mind as much as the more serious ones I knew I should be thinking. The book didn't matter. What it stood for did. Richard Taylor had won the prize. You know? He was the outstanding senior, scholastically, athletically, and in extra-curricular activities. The principal, he said so.

"So I moved up the aisle toward the platform, hearing the applause and just half-seeing the hands come together to make the noise. The clapping was furious. Well, I thought, it should be. If these people could only know how much it had taken, for me, to get that book. Know about the grinding at night and the beating I took in football and basketball. The strain, Redwine, about what you asked, being one of the gang, and yet—not too much . . .

"I got to admit I wanted bad to show them. And I had.

"But, as I stepped up on the platform and the principal reached for my hand, the damn applause was too loud. It was louder than for anybody else. Why? I knew why, man.

"And I wanted all of a sudden to turn on them clapping down there and scream at them, 'Yes, you white bastards, this *is* pretty good, for a nigger!'

"But," he said, in a minute, "I didn't. That unfair thought passed. I took Anne to the prom, and we had a wonderful time. And, since, I've been convincing myself they didn't mean it that way."

We sat in Little Dick's room. Horsehead fooled with the saddle; the silver tips made a chinking noise.

"The reason I asked," I said at last, "this has been a new experience for me, at Liberty, being with all kinds of guys."

"And all colors, too?"

"Yo. I know you won't get riled, you never do, but, well, I clean forget about it, with you. Yet I have a lot of trouble, otherwise. It seems I tense up something terrible—like when you're walking on the beach, you know, and a bunch of guys come walking from the other way, and you stick your chest out and your fists want to double up and you pretend to look away when you pass, but you're nervous, and you would slash out and fight them if they made a move. Uh? And when I see a nigger—excuse me—you see what I mean, boy—it comes over me, and I feel all unnatural and halfway scared of him and on my guard, and I guess he feels the same. It's better with Mexicans, because I am with them all the time, and I know them, and I understand, and I have loved some of them. Still, I know I shouldn't feel so superior to them as I do, but I can't help it much, when I get back down there. I'm Redwine, they're Mexicans.

"But it's the same for other colored folks. I mean, besides Negroes. I can't tell a Jap from a Chinaman from an I don't know what and I feel bad about it. It's a hell of a thing, Dick, but I still haven't got over the way I was brought up—and still whenever I see a Chinese I get the wild urge to slant up my eyes and prance up and down and sing-song made-up Chinaman talk like we used to do with a Chinese man in Javalina. It's hard to tell you about."

Horsehead played happily with the saddle. Dick smiled.

We sat for a while more.

62

"It's just that—" I said, "that now I've gone and got myself all screwed up inside over this little Chinese girl in town—you don't know her—Vera—and I keep wanting to take her out, and she's got me so intrigued I'm going nuts, and I think I hate her. And it's not only sex, I don't think, but just to talk to her. What is she really like? Why's she like she is for? Is she really all that different? It's tearing me up, Dick."

"So?"

"Well, hell, can you feature it? Me with a Chinese girl? Or whatever she is, I'm not sure. I just hang around in town and hope she'll come in when I am. And then I don't even go to the party nights any more, I'm afraid she'll be there. What the hell, Little Dick?"

He laughed. "Go see her," he said. "Take her out. Don't be scared of her. She's probably just a girl. She's probably never been out of Olive Hill, Redwine. You'll probably get over it quick, that way. You'll go to pick her up, and she'll be chewing bubble gum, and she'll talk all the latest slang, and be just like any other girl that goes to high school or works in town. I'll bet you anything."

He laughed again.

"Ha, ha, ha, ha," Horsehead said.

Around the end of February Bo Duddley was coming out of the library and slipped in some melting ice and broke his wrist. He had to spend nearly a week in the hospital in town, and Redwine stayed there with him most of the time.

Jesus was hanging from the wall. The room was narrow and dark. We couldn't see the face of Jesus, but he was all broken angles of pain slumping from the cross on the wall, alabaster white, the dull dead color of hospitals and pain. He was placed on the wall by the side of the bed in the narrow room so that you had to look at him every time you turned

63

your head. I guessed they had him up there to show you that you didn't have it so bad after all. It wasn't exactly encouraging, though, I didn't think.

"How you feel, hoss?"

"My damn wrist aches. Otherwise, all right. Kind of happy, Redwine. I persuaded that funny fat nurse that bathes me and coos at me to give me an extra codeine pill. I'm in a kind of beautiful orbit around a soft pink cloud. It's like my wrist was all I really felt, like it was the payload, beeping signals I'm not receiving clearly."

"You better watch that, hoss."

It was a pleasant, still, soundless Sunday, and it was good to be in the quiet room.

"It gives me a chance to think, Redwine," Bo said.

"That's about all you've done at Liberty, boy."

"No. Not courses. Real things. I'm writing, Redwine. Two things. One is my Commonplace Book, you know, on life and people and philosophy and things. The other is a novel I've started.

"I think people are more interesting than ideas," Bo said. "A lot more."

"Yo."

"I'd like for you to read something I've written—I mean for real, not the Simon Arnold stuff," Bo said.

I said I would be proud.

Some of the Iotas came.

"What say?" P.J. said. Without his fiddle to excite him, he was a big lump.

"You pulled a smooth one, there, Bo, boy," said Smoke Smith. "Can't figure it. Huh? Philosopher fall in a hole, looking at the stars? Hoo? You sipping in the library, boy?"

"Kind of like that," Bo said. "Strange. I was coming down the steps and I saw the moon and the stars and they made a

64

beautiful pattern in the night, and I closed my eye to see how it would look then, and—wham!"

"Crazy," P.J. said.

They laughed.

Bo said he was doing all right. He said that the codeine they fed him there was mighty fine. "How did the party go last night?" he said.

"Great," Smoke Smith said. "Yeah. Ended up a ball. We piled into Randy's car, and to Red Lattice. Been there? Have? And old Slugger here got caught with a bottle and they kicked us out. Drive to the Whale's—Turk threw stones at window. Huh? Didn't she come sliding out that window? Man, and about the Whale, huh, P.J.? Say?"

"The Whale has an immense and indiscriminate capacity for copulation," P.J. said, raising up his eyes to the heavens and putting his hands together like preachers do.

They all laughed.

"It was a whirling time," Slugger said.

"Great," Bo said.

"Well," P.J. said as they got up. "Sorry you hurt your hand, Bo. You'll have to come over and let Janie and me feed you a steak when you get back. Okay? Anything you need from the dorm?"

"No. Thanks. Thanks for coming to see me. It was swell of you guys to come. No kidding."

"What you mean?" Smoke said. "Huh? Brotherhood not just something to talk about. You hurry back, boy. Got all kinds things for even one-handed pledge to do, huh?"

Slugger stopped at the door, fingering the brass buttons on his jacket. "Is this a Catholic hospital?" he said.

"Well, so long. Stay loose," P.J. said.

That evening Bo's cousin Spicer came. He surveyed the room. "I see you are in good company," he said to Bo. I think he meant Jesus.

65

"Hello, Michael," Bo said.

"Here. I brought you some books. You might as well improve your mind as lie there filled with lascivious thoughts, remembering the last time you seduced somebody."

"I was remembering the last time I seduced Gretchen," Bo said. He winked at me.

"Sure. Here's a letter that arrived airmail special delivery from home for our precious boy. Full of advice and sickening goo, I'm sure."

Bo grabbed the letter.

"How's Monroe?"

"Monroe Gee, commonly known as Lord Acne, when I left, was sitting up on your bed listening to your phonograph and informed me that I was an obscenity when I asked him if he'd like to walk in town to see his hero."

Bo laughed.

Spicer hovered over Bo. He reached and stabbed a finger to the cast.

"I trust the pain is sufficiently intense," he said.

Then he said goodbye and left.

Bo tore open the letter with his hand and teeth and I saw there were three notes inside, one from each of his family. He didn't read them to me; sometimes he did.

He read the letters several times.

Later, we had another visitor. It was the Mother Superior or whatever she was of the hospital. She came down the hall and could be heard cackling at other doorways before she appeared. She squinted in at us from under her starched hood. You couldn't see her face, but her gnarled-up hands kept snaking out from the sleeves of her gown, which had a sash and some keys around the waist. The hands would rub together and then disappear back up her sleeves. She had a high voice, like the vibrations of water pipes in cold weather.

66

"Who are you?" she cackled. "Eh? Eh? Why are you here? What is it, boy?"

"*Awk. Awrk. Awrrrk!*"

She had a parrot. It was hunched up on her shoulder.

"*Awrrk*," the parrot screamed.

Then she went away.

"You're the hero, I mean, protagonist, of my novel," Bo said. "You are the personification of hedonism, and Michael Spicer is asceticism. But you are more natural, and you win out. All the guys will be in it."

"Just so they don't hear about it in Javalina," I said.

It was dead night now, out yonder.

"I was thinking about home," Bo said. "You've got to come home with me this summer, Redwine."

"You've drug me every other place."

"There isn't any more certain place than Indiana. I've been thinking about my family today. I knew I'd get a letter, when they heard. I could see them all day long. My dad was spending church-time with an axhaft in his fine strong hands. He was splitting the black locust and the apple for the pungent burning in the black and gold screened hearth. We have an old farmhouse, kind of, Redwine—oh, I've told you that.

"The garden by the house is full of somber winter flowers, now, without potatoes under brown earth hills, without tomatoes or green bean vines, with only dead brown stalks of field corn, with some snow scattered in among them.

"My mother, then. I could see her placing silver, and blue china, on the dining-room table. Then Margie was giving grace, and they were eating the pot roast and the mashed potatoes and the tossed salad and the pie.

"Later, they were watching TV and having coffee by the fire in the living room with the endlessly figured carpet under them. Or, they were playing ping pong in the game

67

room. Or, my mother was reading poetry, my father Winston
Churchill. Margie was running to the phone—she and Aglaia
would love each other, I know, Redwine.

"Houses away from them, Wolf Abrams, my old buddy I've
told you about, is in his dirty garage tenderly replacing a rod
in his old Caspar Milquetoast auto. My Marianne is curled
up at home thinking of me, I hope. Mr. Dix, who woke me
up to learning, is probably reading Latin in a slim volume from
a green leather set, smoking a pipe, in his rented room. And,
Redwine, my friend, a tree, right now, is falling in the forest,
and we can't see it and we don't hear it, but don't we know
that it is falling?"

Bo dozed off, and I did too.

Later on I woke and saw the Mother Superior looking in
at us.

"Are you awake?" she said. "Eh? Who are you, boy? What
are you here for? Are you all right?"

"*Awrrrk*," the parrot screamed.

But Bo was sound asleep.

At Liberty we had a combo, up in the big stone dorm,
when things got particularly cold and mournful. Rojo had
his guitar, and P.J. had his fiddle. I fixed up a tub with a
broom handle and a string as a bass for Little Dick, and
when Bo came he was content to play the comb. The amazing thing was, Monroe Gee was the best of all. He played
trombone, and he played it good. His horrible pimples
would get twice as red, and when he blew, man, it looked like
the yellow points would leap out from his face. I had a horn.
I played it kind of like Jonah Jones must of when he was prac-
ticing for the sixth-grade home-room orchestra. But we
played hot and then sweet, soft and loud, "Pennies from
Heaven," "Nevertheless," "Melancholy Baby," "Closer Walk
with Thee," and into some far-out stuff, as much as it was

in us to do. I took Rojo's guitar and did "That Moon Up There's No Resting Place for Me," and they all cried when I sang "Dad Gave My Dog Away," it was sad. Until Baumberg came in bitching we were ruining his TV business; but he went and got his flute, and he was real cool on a flute. And when they all left, I sat with a mute on my horn and blew soft and just barely.

> "I sing a maiden
> That is makeles.

What do you think of that, Walker?" Spicer said.

"All right. What is a maiden that is makeless?"

"Guess, stud."

"I reckon it's one you can't make."

"It goes on, Walker:

> King of all kings
> To her son she ches,

and 'makeles' means 'matchless,' and the maiden referred to is the mother of Christ."

"Well," I said, "that's a pretty low trick, Spicer, and I don't know why you think it's so Goddamn funny, to trick me into saying that. You knew what I'd think."

"It wasn't very nice," Bo said.

"I didn't know he would be so terribly offended," Spicer said.

And so we made it through February.

Chapter Nine

I FINALLY got up the nerve to ask Vera out.

It was at the cafeteria, and I was going through the line, and stopped in front of Vera; before she could ask what my dessert order was I flat asked her for that night; and she looked at me and said, okay, 8:30, at her house. I grabbed the first dessert my hand touched and took off for a table, nearly shaking to death. It was rice pudding, and we didn't look at each other all the time I ate.

I was at her house at 8:30.

Vera wasn't ready.

Her folks were there. She must of been half-Chinese and half Lord knows what. She had a Chinese daddy that was a little old wiry two-bit kind of a chap and a great big old buxom rotten-toothed mama that could of been anything from a Guinea to a Negro to a Mexican to a kind of sloppy dirty whatever, only she was a nurse. She had been Bo's nurse in the hospital. They lived in the worst part of town, by the freight depot and the mop-handle factory. It was just a shack, and the main room was a kitchen that stunk horribly of grease and slop all cooked together, mostly cabbage and pork fat. They had a brand-new refrigerator in that shack, polished gleaming white, and the chairs were bright yellow plastic and shiny chrome like the table. They had a 17-inch

TV stuck in that kitchen too. At the end of the room was a sheet hanging from the ceiling, and then I caught on that there was only one other room, which must be her parents', and that behind the sheet was Vera's; and sure enough I saw that sheet move a couple of times.

I stood there like a stoop. I hadn't really counted on Vera having parents. They made me sit on a ratty old couch, and I fingered a bright blue pillow that was embroidered with a picture of a battleship and the words U S NAVY.

"You just have seat here," Mr. Sevra said, staring at me and pointing to the couch where I was sitting. "Vera be in, in a minute. You know this women." He winked and went back to watching a movie on TV.

"Yes, sir," I said.

Mrs. Sevra was staring at me from over her hot ironing board. She was, as Professor Bielo says, transpiring pretty bad. She kept wiping her big dirty face with an arm full of loose fat.

"How's your friend's wrist?" she demanded.

"Fine, ma'am. It's most healed up."

"Is that cast itching him?"

"Yes'm. I guess so."

"Listen," said Mrs. Sevra. "Sometimes it gets to itching so bad the only thing to do is slide a coat hanger up there and rub them scales off. You tell him that. It won't hurt."

"Yes'm."

"I'll go and see if Vera ain't ready yet. You care for a cold drink or something, George?"

"Who, me, ma'am? No, thank you." I didn't know why I hadn't driven around the block.

Mrs. Sevra shuffled across the floor and wiggled around the sheet to see if her daughter was ready. Her little two-bit husband wheeled around from the TV and stared at me with squinty eyes.

"Why do you wear boots? You cowboy? Hee hee hee. You going to college? What you major in?"

"Nothing in particular, sir. Just a general course."

"General course no good," he said, and whipped back around with his eyeballs right on that picture screen and turns up the volume a couple of notches.

I squirmed on the couch and fiddled with the pillow and thought I would get sick from the smell.

"Hello," Vera said. I leaped up.

She had done a job with rouge and bright orange lipstick and mascara to emphasize her eyes and little narrow mouth and angled cheekbones. She didn't smile or say anything else but just stood there with her mama.

"I try to get Vera to dress up a little more," her mama said. "Vera has nice clothes. She makes them herself. She embroiders wonderful."

"Shut up, mama," the girl said.

"Vera is a capable girl," her mother said. "I wish you would of wore your new dress for George."

"We're just going to the show, mama," she said, smoothing her black skirt over her thighs and tucking at her green sweater.

"You look fine," I said. "You ready?"

Never looking up, Mr. Sevra said, "Glad to meet you. Have fun. Come back."

"Don't you keep our baby out too late," Mrs. Sevra said. "You ain't going to the college, are you?"

"No, ma'am. Well, good night, Mr. and Mrs. Sevra. Pleased to meet you."

In the T Bird Vera said, "I told them your name was George."

"Why did you?"

"I thought you might want me to."

"Well, whenever it comes up again, you can tell them my

name is Redwine Walker. Whatever I do, Redwine Walker is doing it."

Vera sucked on her gum. "Hell," she said. "I don't care. Suit yourself, Hopalong. A real duet, my old man and my old lady, huh? We going to the college? How's my friend Turk Randy?"

We were way out of town now, blazing through the dark hills and by the farm country and the woodlands. She reached across to me and put her thin little hand, like a baby bird's claw, on my leg. When I trembled, Vera laughed. I jammed down on the accelerator.

"Where we going?" she said. "You taking me to Texas? God, yes, take me to Texas, Georgie boy."

I drove to another town and took Vera to a show. She ate popcorn with loud smacks and then wiped her hands on her skirt. I was conscious of every time she moved; I yearned to let my arm go around the back of her seat and over her shoulders; but I sat stiff as a lizard, and once when her elbow flopped down on the arm between us where mine was I moved mine off. After the show we drove all the way to another town and ate banana splits.

She was home before midnight. I went around and opened the door for her.

"Little Lord Liberty," she said.

We stood at the door of her shack. Her eyes were black as slits. She ran her tongue over her lips. She had orange on one front tooth. She was little. Standing there she came about up to my chest. She looked at me and laughed, only it was more a snarl. "What's your dessert order?" she said.

Bending down, I kissed her, not long, not hard. That near, she smelled like disinfectant, and her lips tasted like salt. Through the green wool sweater she smelled ripe. There was another smell of cindery smoke and the sound of freight cars being coupled from the depot; and just the faint odor of

73

grease and rotten cabbage from inside. I kissed her again, with my eyes open, and I saw her eyes were open too, looking at me. I didn't know if it tasted more like salt or like blood when you suck a bite. Then I backed away, and turned, and got out of there like a dose of salts through a widow woman.

"No cigar tonight?" Bo asked me, back in Old Liberty. I had wanted to talk to him, after he said that I couldn't.

Vera and I went out three more times that week. She broke dates for me. Most of the time we met at 8, after work, at the cafeteria, I couldn't stand to go back in her house. We went to the show in town, and finally went to the Red Lattice. None of the town boys bothered us. I drank too many whisky sours. Vera sipped at straight rye. Every night I kissed her at the front door to her place, and I could hear the TV moaning along inside, and her lips were wet, salty, sweet, like kissing the petals of a damp sour flower.

After the Red Lattice, we drove and drove, as usual. The T Bird purred. Vera sat leaning toward me and put her hand on my shoulder. We drove in and out among the farm roads.

"That's my moon," she said. It was a little sliver of moon, just beginning, but keen and intense in the black, black sky. "Not the stupid full moon, that looks like old cheese."

"Take me to Liberty," she said.

"It's dead."

"I want to see where you live."

It was late already, past midnight; but we drove slowly down the gravel road to the college. She sat up very straight, about as big as a second, over by the right-hand door.

We walked up the flights of splintery stairs to Top Floor, under the orange bulbs that hung from the ceiling, and you could hear my boot heels on the wood. She excused herself and went into the head, and then came back out to where I was standing in the hallway. Old Liberty was still, nobody was around or awake; and I unlocked my door and we went in and I switched on the lights.

She stood in the room and looked.

"Wild," she said.

There were yellows and reds and oranges and blacks in the drapes and the bedspreads and over the walls in Indian and Mexican blankets and paintings of the Great Southwest and Indians and stampedes and the sun coming up over the prairie, with buffalo running, and bullfight posters.

The portable bar came out from the double-doored closet and she went in there and looked at and felt of all my clothes and things, and looked at my guns, and took to fondling a black and crimson dress boot.

"Leather is so nice," she said.

She looked like a little girl getting the wrong present in a Chinese orphanage. I took the jug of Jack Black and poured out two glassfuls and handed one to her, which spoiled the illusion when she gulped it. She had on a new dress she had made, and it was her version of the sack, or something. It was a shapeless gray dress that went from under her chin down way below her knees and buttoned in the back. It was pretty bad. She sat on the bed.

"A horrible-looking boy was in the can," she said. "I don't think he'd seen a girl before. He was a slimy boy."

"He's all right," I said.

"He looked at me. They should kill anybody when he's born, that looks like that."

"No."

I sat at the desk. It had *Thompson '61, Niogi '38, Mc-Kissock '02*, and other names carved deep in it.

"I feel good," Vera said. "Listen, Liberty, when I feel good the world is a wonderful place." She looked at me. Some of

75

the powder and rouge had come off her face, showing pockmarks on it; in the harsh lamplight her hair coiled on her head was so black and glistening it looked green.

Her lips twisted. "But the black moods always come. They always come. And I despair—have you ever been in despair? And I hate—*hate*, Liberty—everybody—me the most. You know what life is, Liberty? Life is a rat race and all people are big or little frustrated rats, the difference is, with sharp or dull teeth."

She went to the bar and poured some Jack Black. She turned and gave me a horrible, twisted smile.

"Listen. Me—I'm filled with restlessness you don't know. You think you're restless—here, in this wild room? Only for a definite place, you want to go *back,* to where all this is." She pointed at the walls. "But I don't want to go there—or to anywhere that *is,* Liberty. I want to go where there is to go. I'll be a queen there. Do you know that? A queen.

"My bones ring, I ain't patient. I want to get there, and be what I'm going to be—now! Goddamn you, now! Listen. You don't know how big I dream, and I swear to myself, to make my dreams come true, irregardless of the cost."

She sat on the bed and drank.

"What do you think of me, Liberty? Why are you such a Goddamn gentleman? Get off it. I could care less. Do you think it impresses me? Or are you a secret queer, *George?*"

We stared at each other. I tongued the Jack Black.

Finally I said, "Are you coming to the Spring Retreat with me?"

She shouted out a snarly laugh.

Then she put down her glass and stood up and moved over in front of the window seat and pulled the drapes shut to, and turned around to face me; her hands went behind her back and over her head and the pulpy gray dress was off and on the floor; and she was naked but for her high-heeled shoes.

She danced. Slow, all at angles at first of arms and legs and head, then her little soft breasts began to go stiff and make angles in the pattern of the dance, and she bent and weaved, and turned and danced to the drapes until they touched her, and flowed around, and her eyes were jet and wide and round, she danced around the wall of the room and stopped by me, never stopping the moving of arms and legs, and danced away from me, her face and her soft tight little body and little round belly hot and wet with sweat.

And I rose up and lashed at her with my hand and felt cheekbone and soft chin and teeth and lips and looked and saw my hand was smeared orange. I caught her, against the red and yellow and black blanket hanging on the wall, and then over the big brown leather footstool with her black hair unloosed and hanging to the floor, and I couldn't see her eyes, but her little brown tits stood up tight, and she kept laughing; and I finished and she laughed again, and her head and shoulders came up like a cobra and she took hold of my hair and wrenched me away. She got up slowly and walked, with her rear like sour milk being shook, to my saddle, setting in the corner, and climbed on the saddle, and rode it, with the silver stirrups chinking.

I didn't smoke any Kopar then. In the pledge line-up at the Iota meeting the next Monday, they asked us all who we were bringing to the Spring Retreat and I said Vera Sevra.

Afterwards, Bo followed me into my room.

"Say," he said, "Redwine, I wanted to tell you I don't see why they all landed on you so hard. Smoke and Turk Randy say if you bring that girl to the Retreat, you'll never get on campus with her. Isn't she the Japanese-looking girl who's been to some of the parties? I don't know why they're so upset."

"Stay out of it, Bo," I said.

"Why? What the hell? They say they'll depledge you if you're serious."

"I'm serious."

"Well, I don't get it. I don't understand the whole damn thing."

I went out into the hall, on my way in to Olive Hill.

"Vera is the Whale," I said to Bo.

He stood there and watched me go down the hall.

II

Chapter Ten

THE SPRING RETREAT at Liberty College was the big time of the year. It was the only big time. Spooks and birds and anybody that could dig up a date in town, or for miles around, participated in the Spring Retreat, even if they hadn't seen a girl all year; and most of them hadn't, except the fraternity boys. The ones that could brought their girl friends, or the girls they were pinned or engaged to, into Liberty from all over the country, and the inn was packed with these dollies, and the faculty houses, and the hotel in town, and they let some stay in the infirmary on cots. All the fraternities had open house and bands and whisky and beer flowing all the time; and it was a democratic thing, for the frat men let the GDIs in, and they came, of course; and everybody poured into the Womb too, and kept it rolling there, and they told us it went on day and night, for five days, and the bird dogs had a glorious time, when the guys passed out on their dates. It was a long weekend. It started during the week, and would commence on a Thursday, April 9, this year; and they let out classes for it Friday and even the profs joined in. The big dance was on Saturday night, and it was a formal dance, and they brought in some band, and Monkey and the nurse, Miss Pigeon, always led off the first dance, as it was well known they had the secret hots for one another. They said they climaxed the Spring Retreat at Liberty by everybody that was still able to walk going down the hill and pouring all the stuff that was left over—all the whisky, wine, beer, gin, vodka, and the rest—into this huge hairy tub of milk and then everybody slopping it up like from a feed bin, and that oftentimes a few of the old boys would fall in the tub and nearly drown from the whisky and the milk and laughing. I didn't think that was such a red-hot climax to the only big time of the whole Goddamn Liberty year.

Everybody had a date. Except old Bo didn't have a date, his Marianne back home was starting to go out with other guys, which got Bo down. And then he decided he better not ask his folks for the money to bring her over and that it was better, anyway, with his broken wrist in a cast and that some of them had inscribed some pretty bad sayings on the cast, especially Monroe Gee; so he would just bird-dog a bit. But all the Iotas were bringing dates for the Retreat. Smoke Smith had Rojo write his daddy for several grosses of his product, and Turk Randy was bringing his fiancée all the way from Hawaii. Spicer was bringing in Gretchen, his deb from Cincinnati. Even Little Dick, who had saved up his money all year, was having his girl come. And Rojo. Monroe Gee said he wasn't going to bring any broad and spend all that geetus, but that he would just screw everybody else's girl. Of course, I had a date.

In March it rained. The snow was gone, and the ice didn't stay, but melted, and it kept raining. The rain whipped the trees along the paths, and filled Old Liberty with mud from shoes and boots. It was a gray, hard, beating rain.

On Mickey Mouse night we had the Iota meeting in a

joint session of the pledges and the actives. We had to meet in the woods and march to the dorm in the rain, and the actives had on long blue robes with hoods that tied with ropes and we had on long white robes. The occasion for the meeting was that now we were officially not pledges but neophytes and ready to be initiated in April. We sat there around the secret meeting room in the Iota suite, and it was all dark, and we were wet and soggy and cold, and the only light was a little candle struggling on the table where Smoke Smith sat in a yellow robe with a blue hood to it, because he was the president. And he spoke to us about our duties to the sacred Iota, and all the mysteries that now would begin to come clear to us as we became neophytes and then how, at initiation, *boom,* we were going to see the whole meaning and significance of our pledgehood and that it wasn't just all nonsense. But that then we would understand the secret symbols ranged around the Bull on the Iota crest, and learn the secret grip of Iota, so that, wherever in the world we were, and in trouble or alone and lonely, we could go up to a fellow, that is, another white American, and clasp his hand, and he would slip us the grip, and we would know he was an Iota. What we would do then Smoke never said. But he went on in a low tomby voice saying that anybody that thought he was better or bigger than the sacred Iota had better get out now, and that the point of being really somebody was to lose yourself in something nobler and greater than you were yourself, and that, actually, you were nothing next to the glorious tradition of the Iota; and that you would be purified and ennobled by your initiation into it, and would get the secret grip and the passwords and the gold and blue pin, at a cost of only $45, and then you would have it made for life.

It was a pretty inspiring speech, and Smoke Smith just spoke it straight out and never said "Huh?" or anything one time, so I decided he had it memorized.

They questioned us, and asked us what was the history of Iota, and where it was founded, and why, and what made it the only true fraternity in the world, and who were some of the great Iotas (General Kurtz was one, but I didn't know who he was), and where all the different chapters were. I knew where two or three of them were; and they told me I had better get to humping to make a neophyte, if I wanted that secret grip and the pin, and how that my Daddy would be pretty disappointed if he thought I didn't know the whereabouts of all the chapters (I never heard him say there was any but the one at Liberty); and they gave everybody a hard time, except Bo, he knew it letter perfect.

Then we all grabbed torches and scrambled back outside and lighted them and had the big traditional Singdown. We marched up and down along the paths in front of Old Liberty in the rain, and it was night, and we sang some of the school songs

"The foun-der of fair Liber-ty
Was our bold Eben-ezer Gee,"

and a lot of songs of the fraternity.

The rain put the torches out along the way, but it was all right.

After the Singdown, when I was getting on some warm, dry clothes, I had a little delegation to visit me in my room. Big Turk Randy, Smoke Smith, P.J., and they brought Rojo.

"Come in, gentlemen," said I. "Some sippin' stuff?"

They sipped on the Jack Black and regarded me. Smoke says, "Reckon you having your little joke, 'bout dragging that whore over here, the Retreat. Huh?"

"No," I says, "sirs, and Rojo, you little tool. I am afraid I have done promised the lady now."

Turk Randy tore up his throat a little and made like he

was going to spit on the floor; and he said kind of a useless bad word.

"Old Redwinerino, buddy," Rojo says, "tell me your true bud that you are not going to actually bring her over here then, to the *dance*, and the party where the other girls will be—I mean, like, it's fine, she's been around, we know, to the regular jazzes, Saturday nights, when it's just us and maybe P.J.'s wife and Smoker's woman, and they've been pretty good to her."

"Oh, swell."

"But, man, a-hem, consider: if you bring that mother here then. No end of the bad scene. I kid you not, speaking as a friend and not like these here scribes, Redwine. You know she would embarrass you, and you'd be sorry that you brought her. Vera. Hell. Let her come over any other weekend. I'm sure *I'll* welcome her. But can't you picture it, talking to old Randy here's girl, who's been in a convent, or to sweet old Miss Pigeon: 'Oh, yes,' Vera remarks coyly, 'it ain't a thing for me, my dear, to have forty guys bang me in one night, I just a-dore it, dear, only, what would you do about this, I should write a letter to the lady in the newspaper, even when it's forty, I just never get there.' Wouldn't that be fine?"

"Maybe that's it," Randy said. "Vera's found her boy."

"You flatter me, ape," I said. "I thought maybe you were the one collapsed the myth."

"Idiot," he says.

"Vera," Smoke Smith says. "We know Vera a long time, boy, long time. Been around Olive Hill, Liberty, forever. Legend when I got here. See? Ever come to Spring Retreat? Uhn-uh. Spring Retreat, keep her away, maybe bring her over Sunday night, at the end, see? Not to all the nice stuff."

"You guys been making points," I say. "The main one is that if anybody in the whole Goddamn world deserves to come to the Goddamn Liberty Spring Retreat, it's Vera."

"Goddamn it," says Rojo.

"You want another little drink?"

They stood up and put their glasses down. I poured one for myself.

"This is the wildest room," Rojo says. "How do you stay in here, Redwine?"

"Doesn't," Smoke Smith says.

"Just don't bring her, that's all," Randy said.

Then they left. Rojo was a good boy. I didn't know. I wheeled across the tracks, to her house, and it was pouring down rain yet. She was sitting in that smelly kitchen with her mama and her little daddy, that had his nose on the TV screen, watching an old movie. Her mama was ironing starched dresses, for a nurse and a cafeteria girl. Vera sat and didn't show me nothing from her expression and went on sewing something. I sat in there and nobody said pea-turkey. Finally her old lady folds up the board, with a piece of charred rag wrapped around it to iron on, and goes off into the other room. Her squirty daddy stayed scrooched up to that TV.

I slid over close to her and whispered under the noise of the movie blasting through the room.

"Get the hell out of here," she said. She wasn't wearing lipstick, her face was dead-looking, soft and pocked. She was sitting at the kitchen table sewing on a long full piece of silk, hunched over like a bird, and she had on a loose dirty kimono.

"I knew you'd chicken out," she says. "Your brains and guts are all together." She grabbed me and laughed. When I reached under the table for her she stabbed me with that needle right into my hand, so I sat there holding it and sucking on the blood. She sewed. Her daddy watched TV.

"I ain't chickening," I said. "You'll be the queen. Of the

84

whole damn Spring Retreat." But the next time she jabbed me too.

We huddled there for a very long time, through blaring music and folks' speeches that didn't make sense and commercials about your golden liver bile, her stitching on that silk. About midnight, when I could hear her fat mama wheezing in yonder, and her daddy hadn't budged, her acting like she had grown into that chrome chair, I leaned over and took her hands, that were ever so little and delicate, and hurt them so she sucked in her breath and looked out hate at me, and I prized the needle from her hand, and picked her up by the hands and pulled her over past the sheet hanging across her part of the room and she never peeped or even let out her breath again, and then she went back around the sheet, tying the kimono, and I fell over a cedar hope chest following her out.

She sat down again and began to sew. At last she looked at me, and I had to get real close to hear and to see that her eyes were even open.

"Get near me again," she said, "and I won't go to your lovely weekend."

For a second, I was happy. I thought of Bo, and Rojo, and Iota, and in my mind I shrugged, and turned, and said, okay, whore.

But, I turned more like a whipped dog, and slunk out of there.

"Have good time? Fine, fine. Come back," I heard her daddy say, over the TV jabber.

She was sewing on a dress for the Spring Retreat, white silk like a bride.

Chapter Eleven

IN CLASS with Simon Arnold, he was talking about writing and writers. He was a fine old man, dark as a fallen angel, and he could say some rare things. He talked to us, and it took him forever to get a sentence out, for he would make cigarettes and drink a sip of the tea from his jar on the desk where he was at the front of the room, with the rain outside the high windows that were propped open just a crack to let in a breath of cold to fight the steam that came from the steam racks. It smelled good and safe and cosy in there, of wool and corduroy clothes in the wet heated air and of an old boy's pipe, and cigarettes, and a little thin scent of spiced tea leaves in the room, like the part between the egg shell and the hard egg. And the creak of the old wood chairs.

Simon Arnold talked. He spoke of many ancient writers, and of Sir Thomas Malory and somebody Brown, and said we should read about the death of King Arthur and what old Brown wrote so that we would always have its rhythm in our heads, as a background symphony when we wrote.

"Now aren't you a classicist yourself, and a traditionalist?" somebody said.

He took a little tea. He said he knew not what he was. He said there were not many modern writers, or poets, of worth. He said modern poets forgot that art conceals art; he said that

Frost did not forget it, he was a fine poet. He said Eliot was a show-off and vomited show-off knowledge on the page.

Somebody said there were some good writers around, if you were alive to the world they were trying to write in.

Mr. Simon Arnold said if Jack and Jill went up the hill was good writing, so was Hemingway. But this same kid said, how about Faulkner? Or Camus? Or Steinbeck or Wolfe? Or others of today?

He said, and it took him about thirty minutes to do it, that he could not understand Faulkner, who was cacophony where the ones he had recommended were the symphony. He said that he had not read Camus, and I was with him there. He said that Steinbeck ran a zoo; and that Wolfe must have bit his mama on the nipple as a baby and then felt guilty and afraid after that. He mentioned Thomas Mann as one good modern writer, but got silent as the desert when someone brought up Joyce.

"Do you think this beat generation of writers and artists is analogous to the lost generation of the twenties?" Bo asked.

Simon Arnold stared at him and around the room and at the ceiling, and for a while he watched how the rain came driving straight down outside but how always a little of it seemed to come sideways and splay up against the window-pane. You know he never read the beats.

Abraham Lincoln Guznik came to the rescue.

"You know the beatniks," he says, "with the beards, who would hang around coffee houses and read poetry to a cool jazz band, and some have written poetry, sir, and one or two are novelists."

"Yes," Simon Arnold says. "How interesting."

"But they really do write deplorably," Guznik goes on. "Their books don't have any scenes, although they have a certain power."

"They have this good romantic love of America," Bo says.

"Yes," A.L.G. says, "they do give the impression of keeping their shaggy ears to the rich pulse of America, as Duddley says. They hurtle back and forth in this wretched prose in a wildly longing search for something to be at One with. Or so it seems to me. Well—here, Mr. Arnold, is what this beat writing is like—how one of their novels would go."

And he took off on a beat book:

"Oh, it was a crazy time, that glorious bloom-yielding, crocus-crazy, gone spring when Himmie and I were together. 'Egad,' he would say. 'Poop, poop.' Then we would go in his wonderful amazing beat-up VW panel job. First we went to Frisco, that was a wild, crazy trip, then we went back across *America* to New York, with its lights winking, and then someone said, 'Let's go to Butte, Montana,' and met this wild, wonderful character there, Crazy Herman was his name, and his friend Blind Paul, and I want to tell you about them some time. Then we drove to Alaska, and Himmie was wonderful there, this little, short, sawed-off guy, this truly great egad Christopher Himmalaya that I was privileged to call Friend then, and he was great, and we played yum-yum, a truly great Hindu game, with the native girls and I remember a certain aloof proud girl that I ached for but she would only yum. In the summer we went to Ashtabula, where I had an aunt."

Simon Arnold sat and gazed at him; then he helped himself to most of the rest of the tea. However, it sounded like an all right book to me.

That old man kept us there all afternoon, and some of us would read our stories, and then everybody would rip them up, and Simon Arnold would tell you why they were no good.

Bo's story came in for a going over. He had written a story that he gave the title "When the Saints Go Marching In."

88

It was a story about New Orleans and an old colored man that swept out a joint in Spanish Alley in the Storyville part. Bo had got the idea off a record-album cover, about this old man that used to could play the greatest Dixie horn in the world. Only now he didn't have any teeth, so he couldn't blow; and he just shuffled around in there, until finally some reporter or something comes in and asks about him, and the bartender tells him, and this reporter goes out and buys this old man some teeth; then he plays. He plays the "Saints."

"If this old man plays his swan song and immediately expires with his ancient white eyeballs cast heavenward and a choir of angels in the background, I believe that I shall have to dismiss class," Mr. Arnold says, with a kind of a hopeless dark glance at Bo. Well, I don't see how he guessed but that was exactly what happened; and it was pretty cruel for him to guess it, for I saw old Bo got right saddy-eyed about it, and he read it through to the end real low and fast. I thought it was just beautiful, the writing of it. It had about the curling, coiling railings of the New Orleans porches like snake-black braid on the houses; and how it was at night in the city, and a bunch of real first-rate descriptions before it ever got into the story at all. I thought it was fine, of course I was prejudiced. Still I was sorry to see that old Simon tear it up.

It came my turn. I finally had him one, it was a Western. Called "The Man in Black." This man, in the story, comes riding into the City of Silver, a big mining town, on an old long-shanked, straggle-maned horse. And he is not the usual hero. He is a short little chunk of a fellow dressed all in black, and he carries this book and wears this gold cross that squints in the sun, and his name is Gun Jones.

So he goes into the biggest saloon, the Silver Cat, and there is a long mirror mounted in silver, and a Chinese marble-topped bar, and a lot of lizardy gamblers in there. So he gets a beer at a table in the corner, and takes to reading this book. Then on the scene comes a girl whose superb body is sheathed in silver satin; and she has scarlet lips, you know, and eyes that are ebony-violet wells, and her hair is the color of her dress. She is the silver cat, you see.

But she is interrupted by this young youth that comes stomping in just then saying things like, "Move out my way, damn you. I know Splain is here, and I will make him pay." Then a slick-haired old boy with a scar on his face stops him, and he has a long-barreled revolver with a handle of notched ivory hung low on each hip. He is flanked by two flashy-dressed gunmen, and two others come in through the swinging doors, and he tells this kid to vamoose.

So they grab the kid, and the old boy with the scar clubs him twice in the face.

A rich-timbred commanding voice is heard.

"Release the youth," demands the man in black.

"Throw the old *perro* out," says scar-face.

"Once again I ask you to cease," booms out the man in black.

Then the hands of the scar-face and the other gunmen go for their pistols. And scar-face, that was renowned for his speed on the draw, actually has his guns unholstered when he hits that polished hardwood floor. One gunman lay sprawled on the floor, with a slug in his belly, and another one had a bullet lodged in his heart. The other gunmen flee. A shocked disbelief fills the air.

It goes on like that, at a pretty fast clip. And old Gun Jones gets the boy and the girl together and manages to kill Splain the big bad dog after quite a bit more trouble, but he gets killed by the sheriff, Lacey Colefield, that is an old friend of his when he had been a preacher down in Texas. One good part is when Big Switch and Flicker trap Gun up in his hotel room with nothing on, in the middle of the room in a tub taking a bath; but he just simply hoists up the steaming hot tub and heaves it at them and that is that. So when his old buddy Lacey Colefield shoots him, Gun is sitting slumping forward in the dirt and his glazed eyes look down without life at the red splotch of blood decorated by a small gold cross that spreads over his stomach. A black book has fallen in the road by him and it lies there, stained and torn, beside the empty gun. It is up to you to figure it is the Bible.

"Splendid satire," Simon Arnold says.

He praises my story, which hacked me because of Bo, but Bo just laughed and said it was fine, too. And they congratulated me on ever getting a story *done,* and I felt pretty good, and told them, the blind hog picks up an acorn some days. I didn't expect Mr. Simon Arnold had ever read a Western before, he was that kind of a simple old man; but he did say it was a splendid satire, so I laughed along with them; but I wrote it for the straight thing. I sent it home for my Daddy and Bubba to read, and they liked it a lot.

Well, I went to my classes, and I roamed the countryside, and I couldn't hardly bear to stay much in my room any more, because of that yellow and red and black blanket, hanging there. Or even when I burned it.

I was set on bringing Vera, and they all kept working on me, even Bo. Later they came to realize I was set on it, and stopped talking to me about it, except el gran Turco Randy, and he told me 900 times what would happen if I did.

I went up into the Eye, and they were discussing existentialism, so I left. I went early to the dining hall, to eat the cold gravied meat, and didn't stay for the songs, and didn't sit with the Iotas. Bo tried to talk to me and I said for him to let me alone. Old Liberty was like the tremendous belly of a spider to me. I went to the pool to swim, and left. Vera was there, with Smoke Smith, and he had her around the waist, swimming with her. I raced off into the woods, to walk and shout curses at the trees, and they answered something scornful back. I went driving, and rode and rode and rode. In a little village I bought a clear bottle of vodka; I never had had it before. I woke up in a tree, and I came back into the belly of the spider.

"Come along," Bo said to me one night. He kept trying to get me to do different things, and forget her. "There's a Communist speaking," he said, "in the auditorium." And he hauled me over to hear that creature talk.

The auditorium was pretty well packed with students and a few professors, and some folks from town. It was a public lecture, and a bunch of people had turned out to see a real live Communist that would admit he was one.

He smirked up there and was introduced by Monkey himself, who winked and nodded and cut his eyes around and fidgeted the whole time of the lecture, and the old Communist said a mess of things I didn't understand and then he came back down the road and said them all again. Monkey said in giving him to us that it was the essence of the mission of Liberty College to hear all ideas and sides and opinions presented, and that it was the essence of a free democratic society to allow for the free competition of ideas, and if you didn't dare to hear other ideas against your own, you had better look out, maybe you had some weak old ideas that it wasn't worth the trouble of keeping them in your head. So I listened as best I could, but I couldn't get most of it, and what I could, I couldn't swallow. I agreed with Monkey, only my version of it was that it was real fine to get the opportunity to see a skunk held up by the tail if you had never seen one so you could recognize it after that, and either run or stomp it. I mean, as Rojo would say, I have a pretty big thing for private property and private Goddamn everything else.

This particular Communist was a stocky, greasy character that smoked a big cob pipe. He had a long hook nose, and he picked at it, but not to much avail; and he lighted up his pipe seven or eight thousand times, but it wouldn't stay; and his voice was barely loud enough so you could hear him; and all in all, I guess what he was talking for was that if you had a bunch of other folks to help you pick your nose, or light your pipe, or give a lecture, you'd be better off, and then you could kind of share the results around. He jawed a good bit about freedom, and what it was (it was only if you could submerge yourself in something greater, like all the rest of the people, and then you could be free to do whatever they let you do, kind of like Iota or the Church). Then another thing that appealed to me about as much as the tongue of a gila monster was that this joker kept calling America such a mockery of democracy and freedom and all, and he defined democracy his own way, and he told his pipe all about true equality, and he defined that.

He polished her off, and called for questions. A two-bit pinko from the Womb stood up and squeaked, wasn't it a proof of the mockery that was American freedom, the way minorities were treated? Then Harmon Baumberg stands up and tells him prejudice and intolerance and such don't depend on or particularly improve with any special system or way of economics, and I applauded; but some of them hissed Harmon.

Pretty soon old earnest Bo stands up, and gets called on. He asked the fellow isn't it obvious to him this isn't the thirties and that America is pretty well off and happy with its system and isn't it a fact that the Communist Party is dead as a pumpkin in the U.S.? At that the old fool screams at Bo, and tells him if he had any true regard for humanity he couldn't say that what is at least the seeds of all future society is dead, and he couldn't be content with the status quo when

93

people are starving and selling their babies and not working right here in Olive Hill and when Negroes are denied the vote and to go to school and so on.

When he calmed down, Bo asked him what was the objective of American Communism, was there such a thing, or wasn't it for the overthrow of the U.S. and for the world domination of Russia? Bo was serious; he wanted to know if the old boy really thought he could be a Communist and a good American too. Now he got that pipe lit up, and leaned over the lectern, all oily like your Uncle Harry, and smiles, and says, real soft, how that the Communists are just a party, kind of like the vegetarians and the free-soilers, and what a shame it is to ban it, or to cast a stigma on its members, or to think it is in any way nefarious.

Old Redwine, he'd been laying low. But when that devil finished that one, I rose up, and kind of banged my knees on the seat in front of me and caused a lot of them to look around to where I was; and I stood there, and couldn't think of a thing in the world to say, but wanting in the worst way to say something that would show him up good. But I just stood, fiddling with the green range hat I wore when it rained and Monkey recognized me three or four times, and Bo kept whispering to me, "Say something, for pity's sake," so I put on that hat and tugged it down over my eyes, and I did.

"Yes?" the Communist was saying.

"Bullshit!" I says. It rung out good and loud and clear.

Then I clomped over three or four old boys to the aisle, and walked out, letting them know I was leaving.

Bo came along a little later, and he said the meeting didn't last too much longer after that.

Chapter Twelve

✳

"**D**O YOU remember the girl at the Red Lattice, Marcy Lou Johnson?" Bo said to me.

"That I pinched her?"

"No, Redwine. The other one, with the little guy. She's really a nice girl. I've seen her a couple of times at the roller rink. She hates Duke and those town guys. She asked about you."

"Don't you go for her, hoss?"

"But," he said, making a face at the smell from under his cast, "I don't think she's having any wild romantic dreams about me. You should come in tonight, and see her."

I knew what he was up to, Bo, to get me off Vera; but I thought, what the hell, and I treated myself to a good hot pounding half hour in the shower stall, and I shaved, and for some reason felt like not looking like somebody from somewhere, but like just another guy, and I slipped into gray slacks and a cashmere sweater June had sent me, and even put on white buck shoes, they were glaring white because never worn before, and I slashed around with the cologne, and man, I could of been any other Liberty body.

We drove downtown. It was a clear night. The T Bird hummed. Bo whistled and I sang. I knew that Vera's mama was sick and she was taking her place at the hospital.

We had a sure enough decent dinner in the Olive Hill

Hotel restaurant. It was my treat for Bo, and he had lamb chops, and mint jelly; he loved lamb, Yankees do. Redwine ate him a steak they brought on a plank, it was the Chateaubriand for two, charcoal-broiled and not fried, and no gravy dumped on it. And they brought Bo onion soup first, and two dozen bluepoints on the half shell for me. Then they had tender little broccoli with Hollandaise, and string potatoes, and lots of those long stale bread sticks beforehand, with some whisky sours. We ordered up some wine with the meal. We enjoyed it. Bo ate every bit of his, and I didn't have a whole lot of trouble forcing mine down. Bo finished off with crackers and blue cheese, but I stuck to apple pie and ice cream. We sat and drank a pot of coffee and talked of all the pleasant things that had happened to us at Liberty College that year. Bo got kind of a gleam in his eye and said what he had said before, that a true friend was worth more than gold, yea than much fine gold. Bo wasn't a great philosopher, you know; and he surely wasn't brilliant; but what he said when he would scrooch up his eyes, those things were always true. He stayed in that kind of a philosopher-king mood all night.

After dinner, it was only six-thirty, we saw a show at the theater in town. We saw *Beau Geste,* and it was a great old flicker. Bo wanted to sit through it again, even though he had seen it seven times before.

The roller rink was a big barn of a place, and people whizzed around on it like they were off for the moon. Skates cost a dollar a pair to rent, and we got some and strapped them on. Bo put his on and went roaring off into that crowd. I want to tell you the truth, I had never had a roller skate on my foot before in all the days of my life. Roller rinks weren't very big in Javalina; south Texas isn't the best place to navigate on skates. Now my long old legs wanted to shoot out sideways and my knees kept caving in. Mostly I kept hold of the side rail and let the little kids and the high-school girls and boys and an occasional fat old man gin by me, and looked for Bo in that crowd of racers.

Once a guard comes sailing by, and gives me a smart look and says, "Can't hang on the rail, bud," which infuriated me enough to push off into the middle. I was going lickety-splickety, feet together, like a water-skier, about to torpedo a bunch of kids, when a strong arm grabs me and slows me down.

"Skate with me," it says.

It was Marcy Lou Johnson. I remembered her, and wondered how I forgot her at all. She was a tall, pretty girl, with great big wide eyes that sparkled, and true blond hair flying over her forehead, and she was wearing a jacket and a short skirt and while her legs were not sensational they were nice, and she was slim and graceful as a weeping willow. She has my arm, and steers the big hulk around, until it gets naturaler, and suddenly we are both skating, together, arm in arm.

"My name is Marcy Lou Johnson," she says, "and I would never think of letting a young man fall down on his honor at the roller rink."

"Is your friend here?" I said. "Molly?"

"She was no friend of mine." She laughs. "Although I must say . . . but I won't. I have heard about those irresistible impulses."

"I am the original," I say, and I am enjoying floating along, like over the clouds in a smooth jet, with Marcy Lou Johnson steering me.

Bo skates up to us. "Hi," he says to Marcy Lou. "I see you found our boy."

In a while we shed our skates and went in the buggy to a root-beer stand. Marcy Lou loves the T Bird. "Oh," she says, "it's a *big* one. I think the red is beautiful, inside and out."

We sat in the car at the root-beer drive-in and talked.

Marcy Lou was a cheer leader at the high school, and her daddy was a teacher, and delivered milk in the early mornings, and her mama gave piano lessons and she helped take care of three other littler kids, and that was the only time she had ever been out with Duke's little chum-buddy and he had tried to kiss her and she had slapped him silly, and I bet she could. She was more or less adorable, or else it was the root beer.

Pretty soon old Beau Geste starts monopolizing the conversation, telling about me, like he was some marriage broker appointed by the court, or something.

"You know how I met this big lug?" he says. And he starts in telling her about it, how I mistook him for the other boy, and hit him, and all.

"And when I looked up there was Redwine, in a striped herder coat and a monstrous hat kneeling beside me on the path and begging my pardon—"

"More than he did for Molly," she says, and I am embarrassed, and wish Bo wouldn't tell all this. But he told the whole story, and how we spent the night talking and got to be friends.

"And that is how I met Redwine Walker," he said, "and he has figured he had to make it up to me ever since, like tonight we went to the hotel restaurant. Do you like lamb chops, Marcy Lou?"

"No," she says.

We motored slowly to her house. It was on a nice street, where folks kept their yards.

Bo yawned terrifically. "Why don't you walk her up?" he says. "I don't know that I could make it back down the walk." He is in the back seat and he flops over to sack out. Old Bo.

We walked up the front walk and onto the porch of the white frame house. All the lights but the one on the porch were out. On the porch I let go of her hand. She had the biggest eyes. Her hair was pure gold. Her nose was too long, and her mouth stretched into a smile at me.

"Good night," she said. "Thank you. I asked Bo about you. I wanted to meet you."

I wanted to reach out and pick her up and kiss her long and hard.

"Good night," I said.

"You're handsomer in your boots and jeans," she said. "Will you come to see me, maybe, sometime, and wear your boots and a great big hat?"

I nodded.

"Yes'm," I said.

"Don't you have any irresistible impulses tonight?"

She stood on tiptoes with her lips slim and straight as arrows and closed her eyes and we kissed. Her lips were soft and as sweet as mint and warm as sunshine.

"You big dummy," she said. "Did you think I didn't want you to kiss me?"

The car ate up the road back to Liberty, with Bo in the back seat.

"Nice night, hoss," I said in the dorm.

"Oh, go to bed," he said.

I put off seeing Marcy Lou again for two evenings, but then it was too much. We went to the movie and saw *Beau Geste,* and it seemed better even than before.

We dated then, that week, and double-dated with Bo. He took out a friend of Marcy Lou's, a cute little fat girl named Honey, and I bet she had a little piglet tail, though I never did find out for sure; and neither did Bo.

Bo encouraged me, and I couldn't figure how he felt about her himself. Then one day after he had been escaping a party Monroe Gee was giving with some spooks in his room by studying in mine, I found a wadded-up bunch of paper on the floor and picked it up and rolled it out, and it was a poem,

99

in Bo's hand, written out in ink, all splotched and scratched through, but the final version was this:

Your eyes. What color?
I ask myself as I sit lost in the blues and greens and grays of the lake.
Are they the cold glassy sheet blue under the distant pyramid of gold?
Or the later greens, leaves of water, that drown each other to keep their mold?
Perhaps the glinting gray that flashes scarlet flecks when hit by stones flung bold?
Your eyes. What color?
All of these and none.
Not blue or green and gray
Nor blue and green and gray.
For these are words only,
And words but call colors as colors call for words.
The color of your eyes is an ache,
The ache in my heart when I'm lonely.
It is the ache of hot thin swords
Piercing me as alone I sit and say
Your eyes. What color?

Well, I went and got Bo and faced him with that poem. Honey's eyes weren't gray or green or blue either one, but brown as chocolate. I told him that if he was that bad off over Marcy Lou, that hot thin swords were piercing him, for the Lord's sake go get her, I would jump out of there like a shot.

He got icebergy and told me that what was written for the wastebasket deserved to rest there in peace, but for my information that poem was about a girl in Indiana, and where did I figure there was a lake around Liberty? I took him at his word and saw her some more. Yet, it was hard to tell really whether her eyes were more green or blue, and they did put me in mind of a body of water that shifts color and moods with the weather. Maybe it was the poem made me think so.

Anyway, we had a ball. She was a fun-loving girl. And it was good, sweet, simple, roller-skating fun.

And one night when I had returned from walking in the woods in the rain, that was softening and gentling now, Turk Randy was in the hall outside my door, smoking a cigar.

"She obliged quite a few of us tonight," Turk Randy said, swaying under the bulb glaring in the hallway. "In Slugger's pad. Right down the hall. Too bad you weren't here, big dog. She loved it, and she laughed and said, where was Little Lord Liberty?"

I unlocked my door and went in my room. Vera had promised. She had pledged to me. I had wanted to think of her as Vera, but after that I didn't think of her as anything but the Whale.

Chapter Thirteen

IT GETS hard now, and I am not sure how I can tell about Liberty in the last part of March. It was disjointed for me, and I would of gone nuts but for having wheels and Jack Black; so it passed me by in a sort of a blur, and I can see how it would be hard for anybody to follow. It would be good to have Bo's account.

I can be a pretty obnoxious and a not so Goddamn couth bastard, and that's what I came to be, end of March. The rain kept piddling around, and that gave me the reds. Chaplain Erb came and tried to talk to me about going to the chapel, and about finishing a paper I owed him for Religion, on Jacob and the Mighty Men. He was trying to be so nice and Christian that I finally told him to go to hell, and he went away and never bothered me again, and I know he had his speculations about which of us would get there first. It was the first time I had ever been ugly to a man of God. By the same token I quit going Sundays to the Liberty Baptist-Methodist Church, but would sleep till 2 or 3 p.m. and then go riding in my car in and out all the side roads near the college, with a glass propped up on the dashboard and a jug in my lap. Everybody but Bo and Marcy Lou suffered from being with me, and once I even told Bo, for Christ's sake let me alone and stop tagging along with me and Marcy Lou like a little bobbing yo-yo. He did stop, and I didn't know if I was sorry or glad.

But I knew I was pretty sorry generally.

They started in to ragging me again, Smith and Turk Randy and the Iotas, about Vera. After Vera came over for that nice time with them all, I beat her up, and swolled her lip and cut her face, and pounded her yellow body.

"There," I said. "I've touched you. You ain't going to the Retreat, huh?"

She was crouching in the corner of my room, and her lip was puffing up, and her eyes like metal.

She whined.

"That's what I figured," I said, and I wanted so powerfully to tell her to go to the devil where she belonged. I went to the head and brought her back a cool wash rag and she bathed her face and her cut cheek, and then she sat up on the bed, with the strangest sorts of looks at me, and pretty soon she went to sleep. I sat and drank half a bottle of the stuff and tried to read some Spinoza, he was a mossy old philosopher. Then when I woke up in the big leather chair, it was deep dark night and quiet as a pit in Old Liberty, and just the dim light was on over the bed, and Vera up, and the room was straight and in perfect order for the first time in a month, and she was wearing a gold pajama top of mine, and she smiled at me, poured a new drink for me, and then she helped me to undress, and she hung up my clothes in the closet and stacked my boots; strange and silent as anything, she turned down the spread; then she curled up in the chair and stared at me with the same eerie look. I got into the bed and lay there for a long time, and fell asleep again, and when I woke up next there was a weak finger of dawn from the great tall window on the east, and she was in the bed, and she rolled over to me and clutched me with her arms and legs like a poison plant, and her nails dug into me, and she was crying.

"You be good?" I said.

She moved her head and dug her face into my chest, and kept nodding and nodding and nodding, and shook and quivered like some animal in the midst of making love. And I gentled her and soothed her and she grew calm, and we lay there between the sheets my mama had monogrammed for me with our bodies locked tight but just as innocent as nothing, and soon she was asleep, and her grip on me relaxed, she gave up even the little sobs, and I held her loosely in my arms and looked at her strange soiled little face that looked completely vacant now and, what surprised me most, so old, real old, with her eyelids loose and slack across her eyes.

"You Goddamn lovely beautiful Chinese bitch doll," I said.

Vera stayed with me in my room three days and nights then, and never left that room, except to bundle up in my big robe and go down to the head. I kept gone on different stuff, until we were sipping gin straight, and I thought I could never be virile or even walk or talk or make a move without a gulp of gin, it got to be like drinking water from the tap.

This especially is a blur; but I came to respect Vera for

what she was, and I don't know what she thought of me, I didn't care. I kept that door locked when I went for food, and Vera was there waiting. We never wore clothes and that got to be just as natural too, until I didn't think of it, but just like this was our fate or that we had a job to do our lives depended on. I don't remember we ever talked, or what about. Finally she left, and I slept another day around the clock, and when I emerged out from my room to shave my beard and sit in the shower with the hot water blessing me for hours, even Bo was cool to me then.

After that, Vera was good. She never set foot back in Liberty until the Retreat. She had lost her job in the cafeteria in town, and she took up nurse's training, with her mama, at the hospital. Once she called me to come in to her shack, and showed me the dress she had made for the big dance, but I couldn't tell much about it because she wouldn't model it.

A bunch of things happened at the college and are jumbled in my mind. I tried to stay at Liberty and away from town. Bo tried to fire up my interest in my classes, but it wasn't there. Bielo was assigning a new long novel that we were supposed to have read by the first day back after Spring Retreat, and I thought that Spicer would probably actually have it done, but not Redwine. I cut a lot of Russian. Simon Arnold got tedious to me too. He was off on a poetry jag now, and making us read all these poems, and I couldn't cut the buck on that. He would go back to the 15th or the 16th or the 17th century and dredge out some old poems that he considered just fine, like

> But at the coming of the King of Heaven
> All's set at six and seven:
> We wallow in our sin,
> Christ cannot find a chamber in the inn.
> We entertain him always like a stranger,
> And, as at first, still lodge him in the manger

and proceed to show how much poorer modern poetry was. A. L. Guznik and Bo were the only ones enjoyed it. As for me, the poetry made me nervous, I didn't know why, and got under my skin, as if Simon Arnold was in on the big conspiracy that was growing up against Redwine Walker; and I began to cut Writing too. Then old snaggle-tooth Lucretius Finch was reviewing us on what we'd had, and I made a pretty poor show-ing, he was asking me about Plato's *Symposium*. All I could remember about that was a real strong idea of homosexual carryings-on, or maybe that was another one of Plato's. So all I could think of to counter Lucretius Finch with, was, what did Socrates have to say about the Bible, did he believe in it? And that sharp-tongue boy cut into me pretty bad for that, and made me smart and look bad in front of Bo and the others; but I didn't dare to cut his class.

Everybody was restless, and keyed up, and ready to rip into each other, with the rain and the muck it made, and it seemed it would never warm up and be spring; but just the sheer being there at Liberty cooped up in that big old leak-ing, stinking, creaking, dark dormitory was what did it most.

To show you how bad it got. Smoke Smith had been on a tear, drinking and cursing and ripping around, giving us neo-phytes a terrible time, and especially me, and Bo because he was a loyal friend and when you got right down to it didn't care if there were a million Whales. Smoke comes charging in one day and announces that he had called a special meet-ing of our dorm section up in the Eye. Anybody could do that, it had a long tradition going back more than a hundred years, for the students to use the Eye as a meeting or a con-ference room to iron out their troubles and their gripes.

Smoke's gripe, that he was so mad about he could hardly "Huh" his way through it, concerned what he called the filthy scrawls in the head. He had a point, they were getting worse and worse, or better and better, whichever way you saw it; for the drawing was near professional and somebody kept writing clever lines of poetry on the walls of the john. I kind of felt it was a talent somebody had, I didn't know who, and while I was always amazed that anybody would want to rack his mind to do something like that or be perverted enough to do it, I considered that as long as people did such things, that certainly was the place for it.

For a second I thought Smoke Smith imagined I was the wall artist, and I was about to knock him whompey-jawed. But it wasn't me he was after. It was Horsehead and Little Dick.

"Say," Bo told him, "get serious."

"What you mean, serious? Who else but that sneaking freak—Horsehead? Huh? Sure. That little coon probably does it too. That crazy ugly loon and that little nigger are a pair. Listen, Walker, I know niggers. Yeah. Horsehead and that nigger. That wall-writing, huh? That's a freaky or a nigger thing to do."

Bo stares at him, real shocked, and I can see Bo's mind working in his head like a great old threshing machine, and he is wiping his glasses, which is a dangerous sign that he is going to make some pronouncement, and of course he is within about an inch of being depledged.

"Better cool down, hoss, and get all that kind of talk over before the Eye. The Eye ain't a place for that," I told Smoke Smith before Bo got his mouth to working. I should of told Smith right there that he was a stupid son of a bitch, and I have regretted that I didn't many times.

"Oh, funsie," Monroe Gee says. "Just think, I'll get to be in a meeting with big fraternity men!"

So we had a meeting, up in the Eye, after we had petitioned Monkey for the right, so everybody else would stay out of there. Harmon Baumberg wanted to sell tickets, he told Smith he thought we could make a lot of money with such a hot issue. Monroe Gee thought it was a lark, and he reproduced the drawings and the mottoes from the walls of the head onto big posters and he had them set up all around the Eye and stuck up in the window seats and marked Exhibit A and B and so on. Bo and I talked to Little Dick. He was deeply dismayed and hurt that anybody thought it was Horsehead; we didn't tell him what Smith had said concerning him. He took my car, and Horsehead sitting up grinning because of the big treat in it, and they went off driving, and stayed gone about an hour. When they got back, Little Dick laid the keys in my hand and said, "He didn't do it. I knew he didn't." And he brought Horsehead along to the meeting in the Eye, and Horsehead sat there biting his rubbery lips, because he had promised Dick not to cry.

Smoke Smith was nervous as a cat. He smoked a pack of gaspers just waiting for everybody to arrive. Slugger was there too, he lived near us, and Rojo, for Iotas. And Bo and me, but we weren't on his side. Smoke led off with a statement of the situation, and then how he wanted to objectively find out who was doing it, and to put a stop to it, since no decent person would do a thing like that, and it was a pretty bad thing to have to give consideration to obscene pictures and invitations and slogans every time nature called. He said he wasn't naming names, but he had his ideas who was responsible, and he looked at Horsehead pretty hard, and Little Dick, and said he would have the truth.

Next Abraham Lincoln Guznik rose up and made a stirring speech about freedom of expression, no matter what or where, and its necessity, even on this level; and said that there was an inherent right to write john sayings on john walls, and he quoted something from Milton that I can't pronounce it, let alone write it down.

Harmon Baumberg clapped like hell when Guznik finished.

Smoke Smith said they had dirty minds and must enjoy seeing that stuff, and look forward to the new ones, and pray for extra chances to go to the head.

When Baumberg observed that Smoke was a stupid son of a bitch I had to restrain Smoke and Slugger.

Little Dick stood up. But Monroe Gee demanded the floor first. He said once in a bar head, in Massachusetts, he had seen on a beautiful white tile wall one lonely inscription, and it was: *Rena Grogan is a horse's ass.* He said he had given it deep reflection, wondering who Rena Grogan was, and imagining dozens of different Rena Grogans in hundreds of different situations, and wondering what could of driven some poor frustrated fool in that place in a bar in Massachusetts to unload his sorrow and his grief by writing that on the wall. He said it had inspired him to keep a notebook of all such sayings that he had seen since. He had, he said, a little talent for drawing, and quite a good store of these poems and sayings and little invitations stored up still in his notebooks, and he was glad to share them with us, and he hoped we would continue to enjoy them, because he would certainly keep on slapping them up there; and he thanked Smoke Smith for this lovely recognition, of calling a special meeting in the Eye, and then he bowed his death's skull of a head with the black eyebrowline growing straight over his nasty nose; and he offered us all his little private symbol; and he walked out.

That was that. For some reason Smoke and them left Monroe Gee alone.

Then what else happened.

Well, one night, after a not-quite spring day, Bo and I were reading in my room when out the window we heard this "Haroo roo roo."

Pretty quick there a bunch of boys gathered outside, and you could hear it louder and louder and fuller and more and more: "Roo haroo roo haroo," they said. Then they joined in from both Top and Low Floors, and Turk Randy came running, rousing everybody up, and tells me I had better get on my boots and Bo his shoes, says they're harooing.

We went outside and before long a crowd is there, haroo-roo-rooing like a little bird chirp, only it kept getting louder and louder, and by then most of the Low Floor boys have assembled across the line of the middle path facing the Top Floor guys, chirping back at them, and all the mid-floor guys are in their windows shouting down "No!"

Some of the guys have got so bored and hungry inside, and tired of the whole damn thing, they have begun the chirping. And it is the ancient war call between Top and Low in Old Liberty. And I know just how they felt; sitting in my room reading I was about to scream. And I start going "roooo," and soon even Bo joins in, and Baumberg and Gee and some of them run to lock themselves in their rooms.

Then it stops.

You look down the path and there comes Monkey. He is hopping along the path to us. It is evening, twilight, and you can see that Monkey is wearing a morning suit with tails, and he has got a top hat and spats and the whole regular outfit, and is carrying a long black umbrella.

He stops between the gangs of boys, and Turk Randy goes forward and so does some boy that is chief of a fraternity downstairs, and Monkey tries to mediate between them. But it is only traditional for him to come and try that, and a custom, and part of the fun. So in a while Monkey tips his hat to one and all, and waves with his umbrella, and turns around and skips back down the path again.

The chirping starts again, and grows fierce. Suddenly Randy strips to the waist and lets out a whoop and somebody across the path gives a shout and boys come rushing at each other, and Slugger and Rojo are with Randy, and I can hear them pounding along and hear them yelling because I am right there with them. And the free-for-all begins.

It went on most of the night until we were so worn down we had to quit, and then one or two or a bunch of boys would get up strength again and go back to it, jumping boys up in the dorm that had already gone to bed. The fighting raged back and forth, inside and out, and Miss Pigeon had a lot of broken bones and bloody noses and black eyes and lumps to look at in the morning.

I stove up my left hand, jabbing at somebody when we carried it into the fraternity suites, and we managed to break up almost everything on the first floor. But they did the same for us, and it got to be man to man fighting and wrestling up and down the stairs, and what happened mainly at the end was that both gangs met and swept into the Womb part, and that was where things were busted up the worst. Bo got his wrist hurt again. Some guys dragged Horsehead out and held him upside down in a shower until he nearly drowned. They shouldn't of done it, but you lose track of what you're doing in a scene like that. The only boy that was seriously hurt was a Womb kid named Something Sikh, that got clouted on the head by a hard wad of wet toilet paper somebody threw. He got a concussion, and all he was doing was trying to stay out of it.

Another night there was a knock on my door and when I went to open it, it was Marcy Lou.

She was smiling at me, and then was in my room and curled up on my bed before I could think of anything to say.

Then her smile turned off, and she looked pretty sad.

"Do you remember me?" she said.

"Yes," I said. "I'm happy to see you, Marcy Lou."

"I asked Bo," she said, "if you were taking anybody to the Spring Retreat, and he said he didn't know. I thought you would be bringing somebody from home. I almost hoped you were. But he said no. Bo said he thought you had been going to bring somebody, but he didn't know whether you were or not any more. Oh, Redwine, what's the matter with me? I'd be so proud!"

Once I had asked Marcy Lou, as casual and offhand as I could, if she knew Vera Sevra, and she said, oh, she was a terrible woman, but that she had always been sorry for her, because she'd had it so hard, and who knew why folks did what they did?

"Redwine," she said.

"You want a drink?" I said.

She nodded at me, and hugged her long slim legs under her bright wool skirt on the bed. She looked lovely, like one of the girls in the TV commercials.

I poured us out some drinks and gave her one.

"Do you think I wouldn't be any fun?" she said, taking a gulp of the Jack Black. "I would be, Redwine. I'd do whatever you wanted to, Redwine. Oh, I would!"

"I love you," she whispered in a little while.

"Sweet Jesus," I said, and took the glass in a long swallow and poured another, and then one for her, because she had drained hers too, and it brought tears to her eyes.

She looked around the room, and saw the pictures of my family on the dresser.

"What a beautiful girl," she said.

"My sister. Aglaia."

"Aglaia. It's a funny name. I mean, unusual. What does it mean, Redwine?"

"It means kind of a nymph. I remember one time when Bubba was sixteen and I was fourteen and Aglaia was thirteen and pretty mature, and we were all going to school in Javalina, and a couple of old boys on the semi-pro ball team made a remark about what kind of a nymph they reckoned Aglaia was, and one of them tried to kiss her. Big old boys, and probably twenty. By the time I heard about it Bubba was already down at the ball park where he stood and watched the game until I could get there. One of the old boys was the pitcher and the other one was the first baseman. We got some baseball bats and went out on the field. Bubba took the pitcher and I took the first baseman, because even then I was bigger than Bubba. Both the old boys lived, but they didn't play no more semi-pro ball."

Marcy Lou shivered, sipping on the bourbon.

"You're strong," she said.

I turned away from her and laughed, and filled my glass, only the laugh came out kind of a snarl.

"Come sit with me, Redwine," she said. I switched on "My Heart Stood Still" on the phonograph, and went over there and cradled Marcy Lou in my arms and kissed her sweet, sweet lips. The stars were bright outside, a kind of half light drifted in the window.

Marcy Lou kissed me and touched my face.

"I feel awfully funny, Redwine," she said real low. "Daddy said never to drink, especially with a boy. But you're not a boy, you're Redwine. Aren't you?"

We kissed. She kissed me, and it was a new Marcy Lou.

"Don't you love me, Redwine?" she asked in a whisper, lying back on the bed with her glass held tight. "Be kind to me, Redwine, for I love you so much. Do you think I'm a prude? I'm not a prude, Redwine. Not to you. But be kind to me, and gentle. I know you think I'm older than I am, seventeen or eighteen, but I'm fifteen, Redwine, but God, I love you so!"

I took her hand and pulled her from the bed and took her glass away from her; and all the old Redwine that I had known before I came to Liberty College ached with love for her, and I took her arm and unlocked the door and guided her down the stairway of Old Liberty and into my car, and then I drove her home. I didn't kiss her on the porch, but only walked her to the door, and she looked at me from eyes that were all the colors of truth and beauty; and she turned and cried her way into the house.

Outside, on the curb by the little white frame house, I took my hat in my hand and doffed it to her; and I drove to the Whale's, where everything was quiet, but I threw a stone up against the window and she let me in, in the little made-up room behind the sheet.

Chapter Fourteen

I HAD bought me an old five-string banjo and I was sitting up in the room trying to make it go. Finally it did "Blue Moon of Kentucky" good enough; but then that made me sad, and I hunched up on that window seat and watched the measly moon and the ink-black sky crowded by the tops of trees and I slowed her down to a plunk.

"Telephone, babe." Little Dick stuck his head in the door. I put the banjo on the bed and strolled down the hall to the telephone hitched on the wall. The connection was always bad.

It was Rojo calling. "Jesus Christ," he says. "Get in here. The pool hall. They got Bo in there—"

Bo hadn't devoted any time to Monroe Gee for a while so he had gone in town with him.

"Rojo? What say? Where at? Who got Bo?"

"Duke. You know? When I broke the gui—"

"Yo."

"I'm going over—to the pool hall." Rojo hung up.

I stood in the hall and bellowed for Smoke Smith, and for Slugger and Turk Randy, then went to Randy's room. He was sacked out. I woke him up. Slugger came in, and Little Dick was at the door.

"Some townies got Bo," I said to Randy and Slugger. "Come on."

"Where?" Randy said.

"In the pool hall."

"There's six or seven pool halls in town," Randy said.

"Come on. Rojo called. He's going over to help—"

"He's a damn fool," Turk Randy said.

I stared at him.

"Let's call the police," Slugger said. "I'll call them and they can get there before we can—wherever it is."

"We can find it, if you *move*."

"Don't get upset," Randy said. "Rojo's probably had a few. Bo can take care of himself, I guess. Slugger could call the police—but that would get the boys in trouble. Wait a while and see if they don't get back." He lay back down on his pad.

Slugger stood there with his head up his precious ass.

"God knows," I said.

Randy flipped over on the bed. "Calm, stud," he said. "You expect me to take on a whole mob of townies for Bo Duddley? Forget it, Walker."

"I'll go," Little Dick said.

We went. I dug in my closet first and Little Dick drove the T Bird while I got ready.

"Be careful with that thing," he said, but he drove her fast and good.

In Olive Hill we disregarded every light and stop sign and

drove down the street by the Red Lattice first, where there was a pool hall. I ran in, but there were only some old men in there. We spun along the main drag, by Dutch's. Upstairs over a drugstore was a place that said Dominoes and Billiards. I charged up there.

That was it. There was a good crowd of them. Duke was there. He was holding Rojo in a nelson over a billiard table. Some guy was holding Bo. Duke's little buddy was working on him. Another had Monroe Gee pulled to the floor by his necktie. Monroe's Adam's apple was going like sixty and he was saying "Oh, Goddamn. Goddamn you bastards, goddamn you bastards, goddamn—"

I hit the room at a run. One turned when I came in. I cracked him with the butt of my gun and slammed him into a green-topped table. I let go a blast that ripped out the whole big glass window where it said Dominoes and Billiards. It fell like a million bells into the street below.

They gave me their attention, and I levered that thing, and they could see I had a .12-gauge sawed-off and I would of put a hole in any of them. They let go of Bo and Rojo and Gee, all slow-motion-like.

Bo picked up his glasses. His face was bruised and cut. Monroe Gee ran like hell past me down the stairs; Bo and Rojo went around me; then we were all racing to the car. We broke through a clot of people on the street where the glass was; and we drove off.

We took Bo to the infirmary, and waited while Miss Pigeon daubed him, and she never asked a thing, she was a wise old woman. We motored around to Old Liberty and got out and went up to my room and had a good stiff drink, and then I went and hid my car away in the woods, in the barn of an old man I knew.

At Turk Randy's door, I could hear him snoring in his room.

I went in the dark room. I could see, just, by the light from the hall. Turk Randy was lying on his bed rolled up like a cat.

I went and lit a snake-neck lamp on the table. I touched him on the shoulder.

"Hey?"

"Randy."

"Who's that? Huh? Christ's sake—"

"Redwine Walker, Randy."

Rolling over he put his big feet on the floor and looked at me.

"What the hell, Walker."

"Get up."

He did. The sleep left his eyes; he was big; Turk Randy.

I unbuckled my belt and took the beautiful blue and gold pledge button of the Iota out of the buckle hole where I had worn it every day since I had pledged. I tossed it so it thudded off his hairy chest. It dropped on the floor, and never bounced.

"There's your brotherhood," I said.

"Big dog."

"Hoss."

He came, awkward and graceful, like a bear or a gorilla would.

My belt whipped out and cut him across the head so there appeared a long purple line and a spray of blood over one eye and across his nose. He came again, with the eye closed. He caught me in the ribs, but the belt slashed again, a hard thick leather belt. He screamed, then. I took the hair of his head and jerked him around and drove the sharp toe of my boot into his rear; and he crashed against the bed, and lay there writhing, clutching at his face and rear. I couldn't be sorry, but only glad I hadn't used the buckle.

The rest of the night I spent outside. I heard all the sounds of the night and tried to understand what they were saying. An animal started in a field, an owl scared me good. Later I slept curled in a bed of honeysuckle. It was cold and towards sunup it rained; but I would rather of been out there than warm or dry.

Chapter Fifteen

NOW I was alone again—but for Bo.

The next morning, after the police left Liberty, I had a visit from Monkey and old Gilly, the janitor.

"I can't imagine whom they were searching for," said Monkey, his eyes sparkly and amused. "Nobody was hurt very badly—a matter of a broken nose and damage to an establishment." He sat in the chair like it was a fire-ant hill.

"I told them fellas we ain't had anybody from Texas, that would be as incredible-looking as they described, up here for twenty-five years," Gilly said.

"Yes, sir."

"I have never had the occasion to mention this to you," Monkey told me, scattering a gusher of ashes around him, "but your father was here, Mr. Walker, at the same time that I was a Liberty lad. Oh, yes. He possessed a large white Packard convertible. I recall rather clearly that he drove it up the front steps and wedged it in the front door of the Olive Hill

Hotel in a magnificent attempt to drive it into the lobby. I can remember that so vividly because I happened to be in the front seat at the time."

"Yes, sir."

"Don't have anything on your hip, do you, boy?" old Gilly said, after Monkey had left.

"Not exactly there," I said; but I wheeled out the bar; and we had a congenial half-hour or so, except that Gilly was a main one always getting on me about Vera. He despised her.

Also I had a lovely visit from Smoke Smith.

"Gone berserk?" he shouted. "Like to killed Turk Randy. Beat him while he sleeping. Yeah? Goddamn dirty, you. Huh? Listen—you through around the Iota—hear? Hear? You can—"

"That was the message."

"Just have you a big fine swell time in the Womb, boy. Sure. We'll kill you, come into the suite—see? Or bring the whore to the Retreat. See? I mean, we crucify you, Walker.

"Yeah," Smoke Smith said. "Big man. Use a belt. Well, have a nice time, now—your little friends, the fags, and the creeps, you'll love them. Yeah. Horsehead and the nigger. Swell. Horsehead, that's the one. About right for you."

"I would rather have him for a brother than you for a dog."

When I saw Rojo, he said, "What say, man?" and looked away and kind of hurried off.

Bo came in to thank me. "But, I can't depledge," he said. "If it had been you in there, you know, I would of done the same," he said. "But it was me, Redwine. I can't depledge on account of me, can I?"

"I know," I said to him. "Of course not. It's all right, Bo. Hell's fire, it was me and Randy. I was fed up, anyway."

I wrote my Daddy, just the bare fact that I had quit Iota;

118

it was a hard thing to write. I told him Monkey remembered him. Later on, he wrote this on a postcard in reply: "I remember *su presidente*. He always said I would be hanged, and I said he would die a martyr. *Iota no importa, hijo. Hombre es lo que puede ser—y es bastante.*"

Smoke was right. I began to haunt the deep dark Womb then.

I would drift through there from floor to floor and part to part and sit in on their endless intellectual discussions or look for games of cards. They had bigger rooms in there, in the between-floors, some of the individual rooms regular apartments, and somehow the dorm seemed even older along in there, more creaky and old; and for the first time I realized that there were more boys jammed up in the middle part of Old Liberty than on the Top and Low Floors put together. There was usually a game of poker going on there, in a big third-floor room that nobody seemed to live in but seemed to be just kept for playing poker. They had a big round table in there, so that twenty guys could play, and they kept a pony of beer in a corner of the room, and had regular bankers for your IOUs and kept boxes of cigars and cigarettes and warm Cokes for the boys that couldn't go beer. That game was pure draw poker, and day and night you could find them playing.

Spicer would play there, who didn't care if he won or lost, so he did well, and he could bluff. Anybody could come in there and play, they didn't try to keep out the fraternity boys. Every once in a while some frat boys would wander in, looking for an easy touch, but they would get took pretty quick, and leave. P.J. was a steady player, though. He loved the poker. In fact, he spent most of his time over there in the Womb, which I had never known when I was an Iota, and it surprised me. P.J. was a funny guy and was still saying things from such a long time ago that I had always thought he was a real dragger. But he was cool. He never said boo about the Turk Randy thing to me, but accepted me just as natural, and he seemed to have risen above everybody else, and above the Iota and Top Floor and all the guys in the Womb and their million little fusses and differences, and just sat there like some big toad-Buddha contemplating a pair of deuces in a fan of cards like he belonged there permanent—he had been around such a long, long time.

I came to like P.J., and it was funny: it's hard to know who's smart, sometimes, from just being around them, because you slap a label on them, and then you are content with that.

"You North Americans are such bluffers," Cristóbal Gottlieb said. He had lost a pot. "How can you be such bluffers?"

"It is the best thing," a little old boy from Ghana said, that was playing, with a laugh. He was a nice boy, he was proud he had a country.

"Hardly," Spicer said. "Americans are naïve. They are soft, sentimental, and corny. They can't bluff."

"Don't need to bluff," P.J. said. "Man doesn't have to bluff, holding aces."

"There are four aces to the deck," Gottlieb said. "U.S.A. does not have them all."

"I will invent a new deck of cards, to allow for many more aces in the game," the little Ghana boy said.

Spicer snorted. "It's not a matter of aces," he said, "or the high cards, the kings and queens and jacks. It's all the cards in the deck and how they go together."

"It is in poker, aces," P.J. said.

I opened.

"Bridge is a better game," Spicer said.

"It's high cards in any games," P.J. said, laying down and raking in. "Aces are bombs."

"What I mean, to apply it to the game of life, as it were" (Spicer had developed this nasty habit of as-it-wereing) "was to play it according to the known great ideas and meanings of life, and not just by power, for the sake of competing. That's nigger bridge—excuse me," he said to the Ghana boy. "I mean, it's not much above the coon-can level. Isn't there a child's game we used to play, called Battle?"

"War," I said. "Stay put, P.J.— You mean Americans, Spicer? Hell, man, why should Americans worry about the meaning and ideas of life? We have it, it seems to me. Everybody else wants it the way we got it. *No es verdad,* Gottlieb? Why not make use of it, and enjoy it, and not worry about it so Goddamn much, Spicer? Let the scientist and the doctor figure out what life is—the average old boy in Cincinnati or Javalina is going to enjoy it while he can."

"That's pretty dangerous," Spicer said.

"It is," said P.J. "All the people better see the whole scene, boys, or you ain't got no America. And I hope they do. That's our big straight flush, I hope. That's what we can give the world. America is a symbol, don't you think?"

"Of what, I am afraid to say," Spicer said.

"Little Rock." Ghana boy giggled. Then he got serious. "No, I think Hiroshima," he said.

"God save us," Spicer said.

"Well, don't knock it," P.J. said. "It is a symbol, of a lot of things that're good for the world. It's pretty damn great, and worth fighting for."

"Fighting won't do it," Spicer said, showing me an amazing 4 to 8 in clubs. "Fighting is old. Look at Korea. That's what good it is."

"I hope it was some good," P.J. said. "Hey, I was there, young soldiers. Swell time. Indeedy. Once, we were in trenches. It was night, and freezing cold. Those 'volunteers' came pouring across the frozen ground at us, on little shaggy ponies—can you believe it?—with lances. It was crazy. Man, and I was scared. Ace high."

"How's come we can't cut out all the hoodah, and play a little cards?" I said. Who can talk and play poker?

"You want a cigar? Pure Havana," Gottlieb said.

"No," I said. "I don't smoke cigars."

That afternoon Professor Lucretius Finch held an open house for some of us in his Humanities class in his tiny trap on the Olive Hill road, and I went with Bo and Spicer and Rojo and some others. It was by invitation, and I wanted to decline because of a sudden violent illness, but Rojo said I'd never get out of the course alive if I didn't show and Bo said it would be fun.

El Finch received us in the living room, wearing a brocade Oriental bathrobe open to his checked shirt and suspenders, and a water-silk scarf around his neck, and smoking a long Chinese pipe. He let us stare and wander around the room for a while, before he served up some dry sherry wine. Mostly the room was Oriental and Greek, with some stuff from India, and black statuettes and rugs and hangings around, and yellow ivory carvings of warriors and fishermen, and jade and such; and sculptures and paintings and busts of blind Homer and the old Midwife and the rest scattered here and there. He had a library that wouldn't quit, and had books in strange languages I couldn't begin to tell you what they were. It was a rare room, and Lucretius, he was out there with it.

Pretty soon he invites us to sit down on the Turkey rugs on the floor, or on footstools and little low couches, and tries to coach us into some illuminating talk.

"I feel I have come to know you somewhat," he says, changing that pipe for the eternal cigarette and plopping on the floor with us, "as we have traveled along together through the maze of civilization as recorded in fable and history and the peculiar thoughts of men's minds. It is always most pleasant for me, and I hope it has not been too tedious for you. We have come from the distant Eleatics, to friends Plato and Aristotle, over to Veda, Vedanta, and Astika, through the sagas and the various universal myths, through observers and lusty lovers of life, men of no philosophy, through dualists and monists, materialists and moralists, and all the raft of pure intuitive geniuses, yellow, white, and brown.

"And, each year at this hallowed time, as the earth finally thaws, and the rains fall more warmly and the sun begins to remind us that life is not forever winter, I cannot help but wonder what my young men are *thinking*—if indeed you are. Even if it degenerates into which maidens you are squiring to the approaching Spring Bacchanal."

We laughed, but nobody said anything.

Then Spicer cleared his throat. I knew he would be the one.

"I am very indebted to your course," darling Michael says. "It has helped me to see that everything is relative to how the individual sees it, from the point of view of when and where he is and his particular civilization and so on, and that there is nothing absolute, and never was."

"Ah," said Lucretius Finch. "Firstly, Mr. Spicer, I did not mean to have you think that I was calling for testimonials. And, I must confide that I do not know whether to rejoice or not if that is what this course has done for you."

Spicer sulked, licking down into his sherry glass.

"Well," Rojo says, "this really is a fine course, Mr. Finch, I have to say so, and it's made me think about and know a lot of things, a wonderful experience, I mean it. But, you know, sir, like—so what? I don't mean it quite that bad, but you know what you require of us, to be honest. The mythology

123

and the ancient way of telling history seem silly to me, and the philosophy seems like card houses. Old Bacon had it right—the idols of the—"

"Theater," Finch says.

"Sure. That's right. You know: nowhere. What about all these old ideas and myths and plays about man and the gods and all? The world has passed them by. Even the old Christian stuff. This is a world that is digging out on old ideas, old forms, now. The people in it are so worried and amazed about the future they don't have time to look back at the past."

"Alas," said Finch.

"And from what we've read," Rojo says, "it's too damn scary looking back anyway, at a history of half-baked ideas and inevitable war and death. Isn't all that great to contemplate?"

"The man who came from Burma," Baumberg says, "didn't feel that way at all, Rojo, when he spoke here. He felt there were real steady absolute values to be learned through contemplation and study, and he said we better make time to contemplate. I asked him why they did not get those thousands of monks over there, and in Tibet and those places, and put them to work, instead of letting their best young men go off into the hills and be fed free for life, and he said they were not about to."

"I suppose people should take time to think about things," Rojo said, "but the ideal solutions to the big problems, taxes and integration here, and food and power other places, and the bomb everywhere, are so simple and impossible that it's hard as hell to give them any positive thought, caught up like we are in our crazy ways of doing things, so it seems like it would be suicide to change."

"Nobody forgets the bomb," A. L. Guznik says. "Never."
And the horrible feeling came up and down my spine and

124

in my stomach that I got if I thought that Redwine would ever die; it seemed unbelievable, and I wasn't *scared* of it, it was so far off, it was that it was so *strange.*

There was a time of concentration or meditation or what-not.

Bo had been silent as a ghost, but he was wiping his glasses clear through to the cloth. In a minute the old thresher started to work.

"Sir," he said, and it took him the longest time to speak his piece, like that time on codeine.

"Sir, I have a pretty honest conclusion for you, about the course. It has helped me see things too, not the pure philosophy part much, because philosophy isn't really about people, is it? I mean, the trouble with philosophers is that they try to make simple or consistent patterns out of a complicated and contradictory set of conditions.

"But I believe there are, Michael," he says, "answers that are pretty absolute in the literature and the history we've been through, and maybe the religious philosophy, which all comes to about the same thing, the life force, that inspires everything, and all of us.

"And people . . . need absolutes. People, I think, are mostly good—simple and yearning to be good—to know what of all these confusing ideas and systems is right—to know some absolute and to live by it.

"And whatever they fight for or do or advocate seems to them genuinely good and, since actions and ideas overlap lives, these same things must seem bad to other people dug into other ruts of tradition and thought—like the Athenians and the Spartans, or like us and the Russians, now."

"Listen to the brave absolutist giving off my relativism," Spicer says.

"No," Bo says. "Michael, I see it this way: social, economic and political ideas may be relative, that is, within societies, but they're like particles that rearrange themselves in one big box that never changes, which is the moral world."

"Oh, goody," his cousin said.

"What are these moral absolutes, Mr. Duddley?" said Lucretius Finch.

"Absolutes are love, which is God," Bo said, "and justice and integrity and honor and courage and pity and sympathy and loyalty. These things aren't just words, and they're not corny, Michael. They don't admit of any relativism, and I hope I'll be strong and wise and have faith enough to live by them all my life. They're the values we've found all through this course."

Then Bo was kind of embarrassed, but kind of proud too, to have said what he really did believe. He hauled out a shiny new pipe and spilled tobacco filling it with his fingers and tried to light her, but Bo couldn't smoke a pipe.

I was ready to land on anybody that wanted to blast what he had said, but nobody did, and we just sat there for another long, peaceful time.

Redwine lay on his back with his hands under his head and tried to think how it was that time me and Bubba came on an 18-point buck in a field of green vetch and red crimson clover and it was so beautiful we let him go.

In a while, Lucretius Finch says, "How about you, Mr. Walker? Have you come to any ideas about a personal *mukti?*"

I sat up straight, startled. I didn't know how to answer him; I had read as much as I could of it, but it was hard to answer that, in the honest way.

"No, sir," I said. "None that I didn't have to begin with, I expect. I believe that righteousness is going to triumph in the end, and in the everlasting life."

"Ah," says Lucretius Finch.

After that it more or less degenerated into talky-talk and a little bit more sherry.

Back in the dorm, Bo asked me hadn't I enjoyed it, and I told him I had always liked old Finch and thought he was nice to have invited us; and I said I thought what Bo had said was real good. And I did.

That evening at the poker table, after he had cleaned me for $60, P.J. actually got around to inviting me to his house on the edge of campus where he lived with his wife and kids. P.J. had three kids, and they were cute as anything. One was a boy, and looked like a little frog; one was a little girl; and there was the cutest kind of a baby sucking on a pacifier in a buggy in a corner of the living room. It was a prefabricated house. P.J. mixed some real bad rye and water with crushed ice, and I stood with the drink in my hand and watched him grill some A&P steaks on a two-bit grill outside. He had a big chef's hat on his head, with some cute sayings sewn on it in red. We were real ho-ho, and of course I had met his wife, that came to the parties of Iota, she was a bug-eyed woman of no particular looks but a nice body.

We ate the steaks and a tossed salad and baked beans, all sitting up at the table together in the kitchen, after the oldest kid gave grace. They were fine kids.

Then P.J. and me went in the living room and he turned on the hi-fi and played some records. He had some prints on the walls, done by a mad painter. In a minute P.J. said he needed some books he had left in the dorm, and he would be right back, and why didn't I just stay there and help Mrs. P.J. put the kids to bed.

So I did and helped her dry the dishes and we put the kids to bed, they kissed their mommy good night, and the little girl kissed me too. Mrs. P.J. closed the door to their room and got us some coffee, and we listened to the music.

In about half an hour P.J. hadn't come back.

"Redwine, will you dance with me?" Mrs. P.J. says, and kicks off her shoes. "That old P.J. never dances with me," she says.

"Yes, ma'am," I said, "if you want to."

So we danced around the living room. Mrs. P.J. moved in closer. She wouldn't let me hardly dance at all.

"How old do you think I am, Redwine?" she said.

"I don't know, ma'am."

"You ma'am me. I'm only twenty-five, Redwine."

Then she says, "P.J. isn't coming back."

I looked into her pop eyes.

In a while I said, "I got a date that I am supposed to meet at the inn. Why don't I go over there and tell her that I have got to study."

After she unloosed me I went out the door. That adorable baby was in the carriage in the corner, sucking on its thumb in its sleep.

"Hurry back," Mrs. P.J. said.

"Yes, ma'am," I called. I let her see me walk to the inn, which was just nearby.

The inn had been built sometime in 1700. It was so old none of the students went in it much. It had the finest dark wood to it, and a peaceful, quiet, dark drinking room, where I went.

I sat in there alone for a while and drank some ale and later a girl with ash hair came in and sat at a table. In a time I went over to her table, and saw she had a mole on her chin, and sat down, and had an ale with her, and said, *"Cock Pashyvyatsay?"* and we both laughed and pretty soon we went upstairs to a rackety room in the Liberty Inn together, and I finally made the acquaintance of Mrs. Bielo.

That night, I walked through the quiet woods till I came to a clearing lighted up by bulbs strung through the trees around it, behind a farmhouse where an old man lived. In the clearing he was sawing long logs, over a sturdy horse, using a long two-handled crosscut saw honed and oiled so it sang. I took the other end of that crosscut saw and got in the rhythm of the stroke with him. We sawed big logs into short fat chunks for his fireplace. We would lift the long log together, at each end, and gently lay it in the crotch of the big sawhorse, with just the length we wanted lapping over. Then we would lay to, easy, so the saw would do the work, and you weren't there at all, and it would never jag or bend or rip. We would finish with an easy swing and catch it in an arc, and he, then me, would bend to lift the log along the lap of the horse. When we had a pile just under the tip of the long log, I would swing the saw to him and load a barrow with the chunks and we would stack the wood, working neatly and in rhythm, *chunk, chunk, chunk,* laying one on the other, cross-stacking them for a strong straight pile. We cut and stacked the wood for hours, till I sweat. Then we stacked the last good rough-barked chunks and split the great big chunks, working side by side below the bulb lights from the trees, a quick two whacks of the long-handled ax at each; and stacked that wood, that was splintery along the sides, to the sharp corner that had been the middle of the whole log.

It was late when we finished. We went into his kitchen. Herbs hung from rafters smelling sweet, and we drank cider. I went to sleep on a cot that the old man let me use and slept deep, and dreamed about that buck that Bubba and me had not shot.

Chapter Sixteen

ON THE morning of April 1 when I waked up the sun was beginning to blaze at the high windows bright and beautiful. I rolled out of bed and started in on deep knee bends, trying to focus my eyes on the world. Usually I have no thought when I wake up in the morning, except to roll out of bed and start my body moving, and get down to the hot blasting shower. Usually I waked up as a *tabula rasa*, to use a Lucretius Finch. But this morning I had a thought: and I had a feeling my nerves would itch me to death and my loins would burst.

I raced down the hall and pulled Bo out of that stinking room where he was sleeping. I grabbed him and told him we were going, and when he said he couldn't, it was ridiculous, he had no money, and all like that, I whipped him out his suitcase and made him pack.

At 7:30 a.m. on April 1 Bo Duddley and Redwine Walker, in the sweet red T Bird Baby, spouted up the gravel on the rutty road from Liberty College into Olive Hill and turned south in that town, and slammed down on the accelerator on the highway, going south, and began to sing and yodel and laughed like kids, moving on, to Mexico.

Chapter Seventeen

Eeeyipeeyieeyaywhoowheeeee!

We cleared that first dull Yankee country by the afternoon, the corn and hog and milk-cow land, and in Ohio we drove on a hilly road made out of *brick,* I swear to God, and they had big red barns that said smoke that tobacco or chew this one. We had been this way before, with Spicer, and the muggy Ohio was the same as it had been at Xmas, a raunchy and dirty river, but it looked fine driving away up into Kentucky, and we wished we'd been the ones to come and find it, when it was a new and clear and lovely river.

Bo loved the white fences of Kentucky, and we kept driving on all night, and Bo, he drove some, and lost us quite a bit of time. Later, early in the morning, came a heavy fog in the hills; that was green country, Kentucky and her hills, I couldn't believe it having it so green.

Bo made me stop in a drugstore in a little town where he bought a Red Chief tablet. (He would write down everything he saw, and try to describe it, and how the country changed, and later the different smells of Missouri fields and then the sweet-sour of the Arkansas countryside.)

> "I'm just deadwood on the riv-er,
> Floating down the stream of life.

"I made that one up," I told him.

"Can't imagine," he says.

As we went the day got hotter, and I leaned my arm out the window and sang songs and carried on and shot at a few telephone poles. Bo dozed, or hummed little bits of songs—he knew the first line of every song ever invented, then he was through with it—or would stick his pencil in his mouth and wait to see something to record; and he would sidle up to folks at restaurants or gas stations where we stopped and listen to what they were saying, and then run to get it down on that pad hot; he thought he was Thomas Wolfe seeing America.

We crossed the Mississippi into Cairo, Illinois, and stopped the T Bird so we could stand there a minute.

"Say," Bo said, "look there, Redwine."

We went into Cairo and ate thick ham steak and holed up in a motel, for we were pretty tired. But after we had a nap we decided to see what we could see. There was a scraggly circus going on in a field, and Bo wanted to see that, so we went. It was called the Galvano Brothers Circus. We sat in a tent in the field with just a mere handful of folks that had left the TV set to see the little circus, and watched some sorry acrobats that somehow Ed Sullivan hadn't heard of yet; and bareback riders that I could ride better than they could; and some sad clowns that were so really sad it wasn't funny, or pathetic, but boring. The big attraction was the elephant lady. She was a large fat lady with quivering fat arms, and fat legs poured into a set of tights, and she came trotting out with her smelly elephants and outweighed any one of them. She made them sit up and kneel and do tricks by jabbing them terribly with a short sharp jabber, and you could hear her cussing them, "Down, you bastard, down," and jabbing the fool out of them and all the time smiling up at you and going down in a quivering curtsy with the elephants like she was just the sweetest little elephant lady in the world. And all of them, the clowns and the acrobats and the ringmaster and all the rest, seemed shoddy and tired and worn out, and the audience didn't respond much, except when it looked like one of the acrobats might fall from a trapeze, and the costumes weren't bright and pretty but generally shabby too. Maybe we sat too close to it, but Bo and I came away from the Galvano Brothers feeling pretty blue about what the circus had come down to.

We jumped up and took cold showers at 2 a.m. in the morning and lit out, going into Missouri, for Bo had tossed and turned and itched and scratched and bitched, and was certain there were bedbugs in our beds.

We were through Poplar Bluff and out of Missouri in a hurry, and sped along in Arkansas, and got our first ticket there. They chased the T Bird for 30 miles in an unmarked car with just a spotlight on it, from a speed trap, and radioed ahead, and hauled us back, and the judge was playing Dirty Eight in the barber shop, and I said I'd play him for it, and he said he'd take $50, and he did. Bo thought it was unfair; but it was fairer than a lot of places. We cooled it along then, it was a fine clear day, then a pretty twilight time, and the night fine too.

It got pitch-black dark and we were going slow, in south Arkansas, along a highway that wasn't too good, and all torn up. Going by a logging road off to the left I spied torches burning on a hill back in there, flaring orange and wild and wonderful, and I could just make out the eerie flickers. I pulled off and turned around and headed down that log road.

"Here is something you have got to see," I said.

"Is it a forest fire?"

"No, man. Looks like a Coon on a Log."

And sure enough, that was what it was. Bo hadn't ever seen anything like it before, and it turned into quite an experience for him.

There was a thin moon sliver like the Whale liked hanging bright and keen over the Coon on a Log. The warm night was spiced with a piney-woods smell. All around came the shrill yelps and deep howls of the hound dogs. Torches were set up around the hill, and down at the bottom of the hill was an oily-black pond or bayou where, in the middle, was a floating log, and a raccoon was chained to that log.

Bo and I sat on a slope over the bayou looking down at one dog and then another go yelping and hollering from the bank into the water. What happens with the Coon on a Log is that the scrappy little coon is set out in the middle of the water on that log, and then they send the dogs, one at a time, in after him. It is not as unfair as you might think, except maybe for the dog: the coons are quick and strong and savage, their claws can rip into a dog's nose like sawteeth into pine. A crowd of sportsmen had brought their best dogs from all over the Ark-La-Tex for the event; it was a real source of pride to a man if his dog showed well. We met a man from Mississippi that had a dog, Old Rebel Blue, and he told me I couldn't lose money on a little financial speculation on that animal. That was the point, of course, to bet on the dogs, and everybody did, including Redwine Walker. You could bet coon against dog, or which dog did better.

The public address cut in over the noise of the folks: "Remember tonight only contact has got to be made. Killing ain't a necessity. The coon can make contact with the dog, or the dog can make contact with the coon, it don't matter which." I learned that only one coon had been killed so far, by an old hound that had contrived to swim in behind the coon and had clamped down on him for good and all.

We shook hands with the fellow told us this, and said what our names were. His name was Mr. Lubie Tarbutton.

"They have got some mean coons out there, tonight," he said. "Some coons that have killed their own mama."

Even with the night so dark, the moon and the weird

torches showed everything: the oily pond, still as death; the nervous little coon humped on the log, ready to spit or turn or slash; the handlers up to their waists in the shiny water, waiting to pull the dog back to the shore after his try. Each dog would be announced on the public address, and I would place a wager on one or another with Mr. Lubie Tarbutton. When they announced Old Rebel Blue I placed quite a wad he would make contact, and some more he would kill the coon. That Mississippi black and brown went barreling in there like a bullet, then he came yowling out of the water with his tail between his legs at the first sight of the coon and ran whining into the woods and I don't think he ever did come back. He was only a puppy and scared to death, but I hoped I would see that man from Mississippi.

"Too bad," said Mr. Lubie Tarbutton, licking his chops over the money I passed him.

"But," he says, "I can tell you what I'll do, is give you the chance to pull even, friend. Yes, sir." And he leaned close. "You see this?" he says. He showed us the blue velvet case where he kept the bloody silver fighting spurs of a cock he'd owned that had killed seven times. He said he had some champions, and some black Spanish cocks, and invited us to a private party of cock-fighting he was having the next night.

"Isn't that against the law?" Bo said.

"That rooster business?" Mr. Lubie Tarbutton winked at him. "Well," he said, "maybe just a little bit illegal."

Then, when we were about ready to leave—you got tired of seeing dogs sliced up—I looked and saw this colored boy running hard as he could at another, tremendous colored man, that was a handler and had a dog on the leash; I saw the flash of a cutting blade, and a wrestling around on the bank of the bayou. Everyone started to yelling. Then the boy that had run was left standing, and there were people near him in a yellow half circle under car lights, and then a bunch of them rushed him, and clubbed him down. We all ran down to see it.

Before too long some troopers arrived, and broke through, and one of them pulled the boy that had killed the other big one away up the hill. The other trooper stood over the body on the bank.

"He is a big one," the trooper said.

He had taken that knife at about the kidney; it was pushed in him to the hilt; he sprawled back with his mouth wide open enough to have put a watermelon in it.

"He was the biggest man in the county," an old boy tells me.

Bo keeps looking at him stony-eyed.

I squatted and petted a loose dog, until he hushed howling and licked my hand. The public address came on. "We've had a knifing, neighbors. No white folks hurt. Now the night's entertainment ain't half over yet, and we got plenty of fine coons and dogs left. Next I want you all to watch a very special speckled hound you have all heard of. Now, friends, in a minute here let's watch old Louisiana Ringo swim for that log!"

The night's entertainment was over for me. We went back up the hill and got in the car.

"You want to stop somewhere, or keep going?" I asked Bo.

"Going," he said.

"Well," I said, "we'll be in Texas soon."

Chapter Eighteen

✳

COMING over the border into Texas, we filled her up at the Humble station. Those boys in blue scurried all over the car, and one sang out, "You come back and see us," and I knew that I was getting home, and I was glad those boys couldn't see the little bit of water that got to forming in my eyes.

We took 67 straight in to Big D Dallas, Texas, passing through a bunch of little towns where some fine folks lived, and one mighty pretty girl.

Outside of Dallas we stayed at a huge motel with a heated pool. And, just as we had got settled there, I ran into a couple of good buddies I knew, old Oklahoma Jake and old Quénombre from Austin, Texas. Immediately they wanted to get up a party in the motel, and bring in some dollies that they knew. And even if Dallas isn't my favorite place in Texas, there is no finer place for women in the world; and I went all excited to tell Bo, and he sour-grapes it, and already has a book out, and says positively no party with wild girls, he is too tired. I see he is a little trepidant, especially about the girl part, he suspects we are drumming up an orgy. He says, besides, he hasn't seen any girls in Texas yet that don't have tattoos and that Texas so far looks just like Arkansas, and where are the beautiful women and the cattle and the oil wells and the cowboys? But we go out and get a good steak and buy a jug of Jack Black and Bo is amazed, the way you plant it up there on the table.

"It's so people won't drink so much," I explain and we reel out of the restaurant. On the way back I stopped at a place, a roadhouse with everything from Cadillacs to pickup trucks on the parking lot, where the best music in Dallas is played. It is Beulah's Barn, named for Miss Beulah Bonner, the Bluebonnet Belle. She is a fine old leathery gal and is glad to see Redwine. I introduce Bo around to all my friends, and there's Lester Luther Campbell that has written over 200 songs; and Autry Jukes, that has a voice sweet as crickets that have eaten honey under a full moon; and José Cerveza, the Fiddling Fandango; and a bunch of them, and my cousin LeRoy Walker is there, from West Texas.

"Let's get up a party," LeRoy says. "Where you staying at?"

"This here is Bo Duddley," I say, "and he is a Hoosier."

"And you're a hunk, I reckon," LeRoy says, and we manage to lose him later, he is one obnoxious cousin.

Bo was caught up in watching the singers and the groups that would take over the stage from time to time to play and pick and sing. Bo looked funny sitting in Miss Beulah's in white bucks and a sloppy sweater, like a college kid.

"This is horrible, Redwine," he said. "Each one is worse."

"Drink up," I said, "and be a—"

"I'd still be Bo," he said, "and this is terrible music. Let's shove, Redwine, so we can get off early for Monterrey."

But we sat there yet a while. They introduced old Snooky Oates, and told how he had set them all afire up through Utah and Wyoming, and Snooky sang and played a big happy beat of a guitar and kept her thumping. It was good music, to me. I loved the sweet strong whine of the fiddles and the sincere strum of the hard good guitars.

After a while we left and went back to the motel.

138

My good buddies had a little party going there, and they had some girls over there, across from us.

"It won't hurt to say hello," I said to Bo.

Well, we got shut of that particular party in that motel in Dallas at about dawn, I guess.

"That little girl you had, Bo, was the best-looking one of the bunch. How was she, Bo?"

"She was a funny girl, Redwine. She was all right, though."

"Well, I'm glad. God knows I left you all alone long enough in there."

"Yes, well, I wondered when you and Gloria were coming back. At first I couldn't understand this girl, because all she would say was, 'Is that right?' Finally I told her if I said it in the first place, I thought it was probably right. She was okay. We talked a long time."

"Talked? But she was in the bed without a stitch on when I came in, Bo."

"Oh, sure. After a while, she started drinking that Everclear stuff in the grapefruit juice until she said she felt dizzy and sleepy. She asked if she could lie down on my bed, and since I knew you wouldn't be ready to break it up for a long time yet, I said sure. She went in the bathroom first and when she came out, Redwine, she didn't have a damn thing on.

"Well, hell, Redwine, there she was, kind of smiling at me, and she tried to cover herself up a little bit, and to carry it off by seeming real shocked at what she'd done. She said, could I forgive her? What a character. But I said never mind, and pulled back the covers and helped her into the bed, and then she grabbed me around the neck and kissed me. Said I was so kind. And so I pulled the covers up and tucked her in. She didn't say anything and either went to sleep or passed out. Then it was a long time before you came in. I wrote a little in my notebook"—he yawned—"and it was flowing pretty well. Good night, Redwine."

"Good night, Bo."

"Redwine."

"Huh?"

"How about such a girl, Redwine?"

By the time I got up an answer he was asleep.

Chapter Nineteen

ALL the way down Bo sang, "On the road to Monterrey, where the flying fishes play." He loved South Texas, the hills and the trees, and the stretching blue sky, and it is lovely country, you know. Along the road we ate great slices of barbecue beef with an onion and a pickle and sauce and had a case of cold beer in the back seat. The only thing Bo fretted about was money, he didn't have much at all, and I said not to worry, I would manage to scrape some up. He said he'd surely pay it back and I told him I was pretty worried.

He loved Mexico too, the sun was really there. God knows, it was good. Bo said it was a shame for me not to go home, when we crossed the border. He had kind of hoped he would get to meet my family, especially Aglaia, but I told him there would be plenty of times later. He was coming to the ranch that summer.

Seeing the mountains before Monterrey was a thrill. Monterrey wasn't much, as Mexico, and Mexico is splendid. But it was as far as I figured we had better go, or else just decide not to go back to Liberty at all.

"I hope you see your flying fishes," I said to Bo, as we came into the city and leaned on the horn and never let up until we were parked and locked up by the hotel.

"Oh, *sí*," he says, *"multi feeshes,* or whatever. You reckon there are any whales, Redwine?"

"Well—no, I guess not. No whales. Just sharks, I guess."

"Praise be," Bo said.

"Okay," I said. "Sufficient and so forth on that."

We took a sizable cool high-ceilinged set of rooms in a hotel in Monterrey. The pink and blue and green tile in the bathroom and the big old cutter-blade fans and the different-ness of the place and the people impressed Bo, he liked it, and that part of it was gold to him. First thing, he gave too many *pesos* for a hard broadbrimmed hat in the market, which he wore all the time, thinking it was the real thing. And went to climb the mountains, but it was too hot and hard for me, only a Yankee boy would of done it. That evening we ate up a storm in a dark plushy restaurant and I told Bo not to eat the white wings that he wanted, so he settled for the octopus in its own black sauce. We had wine, and then we hit every bar in Monterrey. There weren't many Americans there so we had a good time. Bo lapped up the tequila sours. He was struck by an old sightless singer that followed us around from place to place, and when I was on my way to sleep that night he was busy putting him in his tablet. He wrote postcards to his sister and mother and father, and then he remembered he'd better not send them—he said his mother would have a cow if she got a card from Mexico, and I said, probably not, but she might not think that Red-wine was any too fine an influence. It was a real good day, the first one.

The next day we slept in. I didn't have the feeling that I

had to be up at the crack of day and prowling that I had at Liberty. That afternoon Bo wanted to explore the city. I had seen Monterrey. So I hit the nice dark cool bars and drank Bohemia. When I got back Bo was sitting out on the high terrace looking to the mountains and at the colorful haciendas of the rich and the squalor and shacks of the poor. He had wandered around the city by himself and got lost and seen many things and got hot and nearly died and come back to the hotel sick to his stomach.

"Hey, guess what?" I say.

"You have found some buddies that you haven't seen for years and they're planning a party tonight," he says. He was right. "I'm game," Bo says, "old hoss, old hoss. Anything goes for me."

We met these old boys for dinner. One was a pretty sure-enough old guy called Bishop Bailey, only I had known him as Red Hog Bailey when he was a money-lender to the Mexicans back home. Now he styled himself Bishop, and had a radio revival type of program where he would yell and shout and preach and chant and raise the devil over the air. It went every night from a station that was a million watts and clear channel in a town nearby. That way he could beam all over the U.S.A. and not care how he carried on. He had done real well at it.

The other one was about my age, Billy Jack Trump. Billy started in singing and whanging the guitar at about twelve years of age and had already had quite a career for himself. You probably heard of him, he was on the "Big D Jamboree" and the "Louisiana Hayride," and during his early phase wrote such popular songs as "Cómo Se Llama, My Mexican Mama?" Then he turned to rockabilly and did a hundred records of the sort that just have one line of lyrics to them, with a big beat and a shouting and stomping background, and had done all right at that for a while, before he bowed down to Elvis and some of them. Now he was tied up with Bishop Bailey.

"How you making it, Red Hog?" I asked, in the bar before dinner.

"Hell, getting rich at it," Bailey said, taking the salt, and the tequila from the brown jug, and then the lemon. "Billy Jack here sings the inspirationals, don't you see, and I do the shouting. We got a lot of competition from some of these other bastards on the air around here, but we're doing fine and we cut the station in, of course. Every night we make a plea, that if the folks out in the radio land don't rally to our support, just to pay for the radio time, we'll have to get off the air and let the kingdom of God suffer. And we clean up about five thousand a week, I guess."

The Bishop was a heavy man, about forty or fifty, with red blotchy skin and a big bull voice and flaming red hair cropped close. He looked like a big red hog, and he could put away the tequila.

"Then too," Billy Jack Trump puts in, "old Bailey here sells his prayer cloths and ointment cheaper than some of the others do, and that pulls in a pretty penny."

Bo was rubbernecking between the two of them. Red Hog looked at him. "What did you say your name was?"

"Bo Duddley."

"Oh, yeah—Duddley. I didn't hear. I thought you might be a Jew, with the glasses and black hair and all. What are you anyway?"

"Black English," Bo says.

"Oh, well. Long as it's something American.

"Hold on," he says after a little more of the native spirits in him. "I'll tell you what, Redwine and Duddley, we need some testimonials tonight. I usually get them up and Billy Jack reads them on the air, but we ain't had a real live testimonial for a while. What say, boys?"

143

"I don't believe I'd be much good at that," Bo said.

"Sure," I says. "It might be fun."

After dinner we drove out to where the radio station was in this little town. They had a huge transmitter there, in a prefab of offices. Some Mexican engineers were kind of dozing in the sound booth. The Bishop took over the air every night from 10 to 10:30 p.m. and for an hour on Sunday night.

An old fellow that sang gospels and healed mental troubles by radio was finishing up, and then the station announcer started in to announce the Bishop's show. "How's she going?" Red Hog asked the gospel man. "Okay," he says. "Me and the wife going to Nassau for the summer, looks like."

"He only has a fifteen-minute program," Bailey says.

"Remember now," he says to me, "you had the gallstones." Then it was under way.

They turned on a record of some organ music and after a blare or two of that, Billy Jack Trump steps up to his microphone in the two-bit studio and crows:

"Welcome! Welcome! Oh, welcome friends and welcome neighbors out all over this great radio land. Welcome to the Bishop Bailey Revival and Healing Hour! We are so glad and happy and humble to think that God gave it to you all to be with us out there tonight. Yes, praise God! And we appreciate your letting us to come out there and to greet and to meet you in the name of the Lord Jesus Christ! Our business is prayer, folks—prayer—p-r-a-y-e-r! Prayer. Pour out your heart to us—our prayers for you and any little or big ailment or malady that you have are ready, and all you have to do is let us know about it. Write us a card or letter, friends. Write to Bishop Bailey—Bishop *Bailey*—care of this station. Please write them as short as you can, folks, just simply name your cause of suffering, so's we can process them *all*.

"Remember, we don't want your money—except if you

can make a contribution, however large or small. It doesn't go to us—oh, no! But only to pay for the radio time, so we can pray for you!

"Now, here he is—Bishop R. H. Bailey, preacher, founder, and sole proprietor of the Only True Church of Jesus Christ. The next voice you hear is that of Bishop Bailey!"

More of the organ music, while old Bailey finishes biting into the lemon, and scuttles over to the microphone. He talks real close to it, booming in a raspy voice.

"Oh, dear friends," he says. "How are you tonight? Are you sick? Are you ill? Does your back hurt, or your feet? Do you have a cataract, or a horrible goiter, or suffering from the horrible throes of menopause that your husband doesn't understand? Are you in any way infirm, physical or mental?

"Well, wonderful friends out there, I am here to help, and to pray for you, and I do, every minute of the day I am not on the air speaking to you. And prayer will avail, friends. Are you hearing me tonight, out there? It's God's night, and God don't want you to be suffering or sick or infirm, any more than a bird. No, no.

"Many of you have fears repressed—we're reaching you in prayer. Listen to me, whatever is your burden, whyever you are unwell. Oh, put your hand on the radio and put your hand on your tumor or your hideous goiter that you've got, or on your cataract that is stealing all the joys of life from you, and I am going to *command it to move!* God is in the prayer-answering business and He's doing it still! Now the power of my voice goes to wherever you are listening—for the glory of God, for the sake of Jesus Christ!

"Has it moved? Write me if so.

"It may not have moved, dear friends. It doesn't move at once sometimes, if your faith's not right.

"Maybe you need a prayer rag, friends, oh, my dear friends. You probably need some precious anointing oil that we will send you, or an anointed handkerchief that we have prayed over.

"Here is Brother Bill, to tell you of the miracles that have been done through prayer!"

"Yes, friends," Trump says. "Here is a letter from a rheumatism sufferer in Hot Springs, Arkansas. She was so crippled up she couldn't move her hands or feet. Then she heard Bishop Bailey, and wrote him, and got a bottle of the precious anointing oil. She rubbed it on her affected parts, and prayed while Bishop Bailey prayed for her. Now she is a living witness to God's healing power.

"And here is another living witness to the wondrous power of Bishop Bailey, friends, right here with us in our studio audience, come all the way to bring witness of his healment—"

This was me.

"What is your name, young man?"

"Michael Spicer."

"And where do you live?"

"New York City."

"All the way from New York City. Now, what was your ailment, son?"

"Gallstones."

"*Gall*stones! And did the Bishop make them move through the power of God?"

"They just flew out when he prayed."

"And did you use the anointing oil for only a dollar twenty-five or the anointed handkerchief that consecrated hands have been laid on, for a dollar seventy-five?"

"Well, it took both for me."

"Thank you, my young friend. Another living witness—"

I clanked my ring on a tequila bottle, and old Trump gives me a look.

"I have my gallstones right here in this bottle, and two more bottles of them at home," I says into the mike.

"Fine. Fine. Now here is Bishop Bailey."

"Friends," old Red Hog says in a kind of a snively, weasely voice, "you know that our work of healing for the glory of God is supported solely, only by you all in the radio audience, that are listening to me now. And we have been tremendously let down, friends. Oh, we may make it through this month, I don't know if we can. We simply need for this precious radio time to be paid so we can come into your homes and your hearts and your sickness and infirmity, and cure them. If you can help financially, maybe we can go on a little longer. I'm not threatening. Oh, Lord, to think that I would do that. I thank God if I have been of help to anybody. But we did just breach through March."

Then he introduces Brother Bill again, who sings the night's inspirational number, for the comfort of everybody's souls:

> "He will give you what you pray for,
> He will give you what you pray for,
> He will give you what you pray for,
> You can get it from the Lord!"

After that, they carried on just a little bit more, then it was over.

"Man," Bishop Bailey says, wiping the sweat off his face with a precious anointed handkerchief, "what a grind!"

"Say," he says later, "that was real good, Redwine, about the jars of gallstones. Give realism."

"Oh, *yeah*," Trump says.

"But why did you say New York City?"

"It just came out."

"No. You don't want to do that, in this game, Redwine. New York City isn't any good. Some little place would be better. It's got to be a place where the folks out there think real honest plain folks like themselves live and do, so they can see you there, in that little town, suffering, like they are."

We hit the bars that night, only towards morning we had to leave old Red Hog Bailey and Billy Jack Trump, they were still going strong.

"Ain't they something?" I asked Bo. We were standing under a street light and some bits of stars.

"Yes," he says. "Indeedy. You have the friends, Redwine."

I knew what Bo meant. Still, you had to hand it to them, full of gall and gallstones as they were, at the same time that you despised them. Lord Almighty. And I hoped He would forgive them.

✳

Chapter Twenty

✳

THAT was about 4 a.m. in the dark morning, still black as pitch in Monterrey. Bo was pretty loopy on tequila sours. He began to fiddle-foot off in what he considered to be the direction of the hotel, or maybe he was heading for the mountains again. I clapped him on the shoulder, and slowed him down, for it was the wrong way.

"Redwine, I have got to go to bed, hit sack. Too many whatizzes. That you, Redwine?"

"Sure. Sure, hoss. Take a little pull at this, it ain't so bad. What you think of that moon and those stars—pretty poor,

148

sorry moon, uh? Say, Bo, an old friend of mine just came by, you know that?"

Bo looks around, but it is the old Golden Horny Bird I refer to, and he is invisible; but when he is up there on your shoulder, why then you know he is there, all right.

Bo whispers behind his hand, "Let's lose the bastard. Any friend of yours isn't one of mine."

So I put my arm around him, and we marched on through the streets and alleys, *hup hup hup,* to a house with a sign out front barely lighted showing a ship with sails sailing over the sea. It is El Barco de Oro. Downstairs is a bar, but I prod Bo up some stairs and suddenly we are in a bright room with stuffed sofas and chairs along the walls, and pictures of nudes on the walls, and bright colors in the room, and a real crystal chandelier dangling and tinkling from the ceiling, and three exits lead from this big room with heavy tapestries in front of the exits, and it smells pretty strong of perfume made of flowers that bloom at midnight on the desert and die at once; and it is late but there are a few girls lounging around reading magazines or smoking or dozing, and they look up at us, most of them are pretty, made-up Mexican girls, and keep on smoking and flipping through magazines, but not dozing.

A jukebox with nervous lights plays "Remember Me, I'm the One Who Loves You."

"What the hell," Bo mumbles.

"It's a finishing school for Monterrey girls," I say and laugh and whop Bo on the back. In comes the lady in charge, a short, plump lady in a gray dress, that I introduce to Bo, and ask her what she has *especial.*

She trots out the whole bunch and they sit or stand around the room, smiling and grinning and cracking gum at us, and there are some pretty girls.

"Where is Fulgencia?" I ask the lady, but Fulgencia has kited off to Mexico City; but Guadalupe is recommended.

149

Guadalupe was sitting on a low couch, but I saw that she was tall and solid and creamy-tan. She had swimming-black eyes and black hair and a wide mouth painted brilliant red, and her teeth weren't bad. She smiled and stood up, she was a young girl.

I gave Bo a push. "Okay, boy. You won't do better in all Mexico."

He froze.

"*Un poco borracho*," I explained to the lady. "Maybe it better be a white girl."

She had two. One a bleached redhead that had cavorted with Methuselah. The other was a hard-faced tiny American girl. She came over and grinned at Bo and took his hand, and he looked at me, and I grinned at him, and she led him back through the arras, as they say. It was Guadalupe for me.

When I came out, most of the girls were gone. The juke was playing the same number. Bo was standing in the room, smoking on a brown Mexican cigarette he had got somewhere.

We made peace with the lady and went outside. It was dawning, the air was green, the sun was getting ripe. Walking back to the hotel I whistled.

Up in the suite I got ready for the sack. Bo sat out on the terrace. He hadn't uttered. I went out there and rumpled up his hair.

"How was it, stud?"

"Great," he says. We are both sober now. "Great. She was from Michigan, it turned out. She arranged us on the bed. 'Boy, you are drunk!' she said. And pretty soon she said, 'Okay, kiddo,' and jumped up and went to her little bucket—but I didn't know, Redwine—I didn't know. It was great."

He cried.

Then I saw that I had done a terrible thing to Bo; it was like I'd deprived him of a dream; after that he never mentioned it; and I never told what we'd done down there, even though I had been there a dozen times before; and I was glad Bo never got the clap or anything; yet still I can't help thinking it was an experience he should of had, somehow.

But he blamed me, and wouldn't speak much; and we left Monterrey that afternoon, heading back, and Bo kept silent, and I drove all night faster and faster, until toward dawn I was sleepy and ran smack into a construction horse and into a ditch, and that we weren't hurt was a miracle. It was not quite to Big D, and it was the end of that poor T Bird Baby.

Chapter Twenty-One

WELL, that was nice. The car was wrecked, Bo was quiet, I was mad.

The police towed us out of there, and into Dallas, and fined me pretty good. We weren't shaved, and had on old driving clothes, and were hungry and sleepy, and looked like a couple of beats, I guess.

After we got free of the police, and had sold the car for junk, and were standing in the street with our suitcases in our hands, Bo looked at me and said, "We've had it, Redwine."

I pushed him into a cab, and we went to a tremendous car lot. After a call to the bank, they showed me a bunch of these little foreign cars, but I couldn't see any advantage in them. I considered a big new Cad convertible, white with red upholstery. But I would of felt funny riding around in that

Cadillac, like I thought I was too much. So I decided to get me a new T Bird just like the one I had loved so; only they didn't have a red one in stock, so I got a yellow one.

"Before this trip I never realized you had so much money, Redwine," Bo said.

"I never acted like a poor Job, did I?"

"No. I knew you were well fixed, and your father had a ranch and everything, but to haul off and pay out cash—"

"Listen, hoss," I said. "We have got lots of acres down here. When it rains we do real good. When it doesn't rain, we pretend like it did and pray that it will. We have a few sections leased off, too. I know what you must of thought. I see what people think, or I guess they must. One time right here in Dallas I walked into a fine apartment hotel with lots of swank to it, and the old man at the desk looked at me and saw these kind of dirty jeans and an old shirt and I hadn't bothered about a haircut for a while and he looked real close at these sideburns, and then he saw that I had on these old taped-up moccasins I wear to be real comfortable in; and so he asked me, in a smarty way, did I have the right place? It kind of upset me for a minute, and I considered saying something, like how much did he want for his Goddamn hotel? But I just tipped him pretty big, and it was all right, and then he knew that I could *afford* to wear those moccasins.

"That's the thing, Bo, it's not just taking hold and finding yourself, and Know Thyself, and all that. You try that, just a person without a thing to go on but pluck and grit these days, and you are going to get squashed flat as a bug. People don't really want to know who you are, and they are scared to find out who *they* are—you said that yourself. They want you to play along and be who they think it would be safe and convenient or entertaining for them if you were, and I even fall into playing that game some myself, you've seen me do it, at Liberty.

152

"But mostly, and sure enough in my own country, Bo, I can be Redwine. I *like* to wear them moccasins, Bo. Man, I don't have to give a good Goddamn if I don't want to. I can afford to wear the moccasins and do anything else, Bo. That's the thing. That's the only way to know myself and be myself these times, boy, because I don't have to care about a million two-bit things and I don't have to let a million people surround me and stifle me for air."

"I don't like that very much," Bo said.

But I never said it was the best way for things to be, or that it was the greatest good for the most people. But it was the way it worked for me.

We broke in that new T Bird like exploding a bullwhip, and made it go, and it was a sweet little car, with no bugs, and galloped along easy and willing to go, and I was glad, and concentrated on the sheer driving. Bo never took the wheel, but slept mostly, and we only stopped to pick up gas and sandwiches all the way, until there again was old Olive Hill, and we had crept through her, and were motoring into Liberty.

The Spring Retreat had already begun, and the dance and all the big finale would be the next night: that was Saturday, April 11.

Chapter Twenty-Two

SATURDAY morning we were all up early, and about half the guys and their dates had never gone to bed the night before, but had partied through the night, and the night before that, too. It had swung into action Thursday and was running more like a week than a weekend. Rojo told me that most of them actually started in Tuesday or Wednesday, or even Monday, or had been at it since the weekend before, and that him and Lucretius Finch had held a nice little Socratic dialogue between the two of them in Humanities Wednesday, and old L.F. had inquired where in the nether regions had Mr. *Duddley* disappeared to?

"I suppose you're still—" Rojo says.

"Yo. And then some. You going to stop me, little Rojo-buddy?"

"Hell, no," he says. Rojo was a wee bit bombed. "Not I, Horatio. Or maybe you are Horatius?"

"Nobody but old Redwine Walker, and I see by the look and feel and sway of things that there is a need for me to catch up—"

"We only thought, maybe, you know, old good buddy, I mean, Turk and Smoke thought, that since you took off, and didn't come back—and the charming Miss Whale, Olive Hill's leading debutante, called for you, R-wine, did she melt the wires!—thought perhaps, you know—"

"Uhn-uh."

"*Yo veo.* Quite right. Of course. Forsooth and so on. I see I am in danger of bugging you, friend, with this continued parry. Well, I can truthfully say that I don't give one, at this point, who you bring to the thing. And, whilst Messrs. Smoke and Turkey-boo did attempt to maintain a state of near-sobriety in the early days of this lovely affair, they have done give up now, and I doubt they will offer you much resistance in present states."

"Yo," I said.

So I figured I had best get with it that morning, and not just stand around like a mocking jaybird and gape at all the revelry. My, but there were luscious tomatoes there, though. All kinds of them; and, for the most part, they seemed like fine girls. I saw Little Dick at the crack of day and his girl Anne had come in Friday on the train, and Bo and me went to breakfast and ate cold eggs with them, and Anne was a fine girl. When I pulled away from Old Liberty for town she was up in their room, reading to Horsehead, and he was grinning awful as a gargoyle at her and just like a puppy dog.

Before I left I announced to one and all that I was having a cocktail party in my room in the afternoon, from 3 p.m. to whenever, and that *todo el mundo* was invited. I saw Slugger and he said he'd come, he didn't care whose liquor he drank. I saw Turk Randy, with his intended, a blond in a real dressed-up outfit from Hawaii, and old Randy was wearing his gorgeous letter sweater with the big gold *L* and all the chevrons on it, and he was wearing a couple of ugly purple stripes across his face too. He told me just to keep the hell out of his way, or said he would surely kill me. Smoke Smith came rolling through our hall a little gone, with some of the Iotas, singing Iota songs and waving crested mugs. Smoke eyed me, and we had just come back from breakfast, and Anne was standing there with us, and Smoke said pretty loud in his cute way that my mother was a Mexican goat and that now my children would be crosses between stinking goats and stinking whales, so a man wouldn't know where to have them, although that would be their sole purpose for existing. It embarrassed Anne, and Dick for her, and disgusted Bo, and I don't know what Smoke Smith expected; but I coldcocked him. And asked the others, what about it? But they didn't want to play.

Bo excused himself, said it looked pretty bad to him, like it would get worse before it got better, and went into his room and turned *Le Sacre du Printemps* on the hi-fi and dug into a book. He wouldn't budge or come to town with me. Gee was passed out across the bed. Harmon Baumberg said Gee hadn't stirred except to fall off the bed for a day and a half.

I drove into town.

I picked up four cases of gin and a case of Italian vermouth at a liquor store, for I wanted a few martins at my party. Then I went to see Vera.

She nearly killed me, in that cabbagey kitchen, and tried to slap and kick and claw, but I got her under control. She shouted stuff I couldn't understand, it could of been Mars talk. She sobbed and wept and called me names.

"Well," I said, "I did come back, and I'm here. So do you want to shut your mouth and go?"

She turned it off in a second.

She cooed and ran her fingers on my face and said she knew I would come for her, and she would be ready in a minute. I said, hold your horse, I would be back for her at 2, and we would go to my party. She liked that all right; and the main thing was for her to go to the dance, and all the things after that. I took a cold salt kiss off her and rocketed back to Liberty.

Everybody finessed lunch and ate picnics outside, and played baseball on the green, and I got in a game with a crowd from the Womb, and it was a hairy riot. It was beer baseball and you had to chug a mug every time you got on base and all the bases were pony kegs of beer. We all got to laughing and falling down running around the bases. I slammed one about 400 feet on a line through a window on the second floor of Old Liberty. When it began to rain and drizzle down in big ploppy cold drops and grayed over, we had to quit. It was still chilly and cold and dull weather at Liberty, hard to take after Mexico.

Then the boy from Ghana and Cristóbal Gottlieb and a real big bunch of us went down to the indoor pool for a little swim. A whole gang was there, with their dates, and I met a lot of girls, and some right nice-looking, and we swam and played Red Rover, Cross Over, and other games, and it got pretty rough there in the pool. We played a game of Horse, where somebody gets on somebody's back and then a bunch of others get like that, and you have war, and try to bust each other over in the water, and pull the top ones off. I had a hefty girl up on me that was fierce as Jezebel and nearly crushed my neck between her big old thighs and like to have drowned me pulling on my hair to turn this way and thataway. The girls were the riders and the boys were the horses. My old gal bloodied one girl's lip, and went wild pushing and shoving at the others in the pool, and for a nice final tactic she managed to rip off this little girl's bathing suit so the girl sat up on her horse with her hands over her eyes and boo-hooed with her pinklets waving in the breeze. Everybody had a good laugh out of that. We were the champions at

Horse, and my old girl gave me a wet sloppy kiss and said her date was a creep, and so on, but I turned her back over to him and they deserved each other.

After that was the big tremendous Chug-a-Lug contest that was a traditional annual affair and part of the Spring Retreat. Old Simple Sampson came out on the green in his drinking jacket with the tiger on it and he was the judge in charge. Nine teams were scheduled for it, from all the fraternities on Top and Low and one from the middle. I gave Simple Sampson a pull from my flask and said, why didn't I get up one more, independent team, to even her off at ten? Sampson gargled at the flask and says, why not, irregularities were the stuff of life. So I ran like crazy, and dug up a team. When me and Iota had dissolved, I had come across some first-rate unheralded drinkers deep in the Womb. I dug out Gottlieb and he was about a two-gulp man, and Jamie Kingdom, an English boy that could drain them down, and myself, and just then P.J. comes wandering over kind of in a stupor and says, what the hell, screw Iota, he would chug with us. That cinched it right there, for P.J. was the best on campus, he could just open his throat and it was gone, and never breathe or swallow either.

We polished off a Low, then a Top Floor team in a flash. Each team lines up at a table on the green, with a glass in front of each guy. Old Sampson raised his hand, and each one chugged, right down the line, like a relay race, and the first guy finished at the end of the table, his team was the winner. We beat the Womb crew bad. Then it was left between us and the Iota group, and although they were burned to have lost P.J. they were still known as the best drinkers at Liberty, and hadn't lost the contest in many years.

Smoke Smith was captain of the team, and he was navigating all right, though his jawbone looked a little bruised and went sideways to his face. He got out in the middle of the path, and yelled for absolute quiet, and made a speech.

The main thing of the speech was that my team wasn't a qualified team, and, in the second place, its captain was not a gentleman and a scholar, and so Iota wouldn't drink against us, but demanded that Sampson forfeit the trophy to them. It was a nice big silver jug-handled loving cup which was presently resting up on the mantel underneath the Bull in the Iota den. The whole crowd was assembled out in front of Old Liberty to watch the contest, or looking from the dormitory windows, and there were near a thousand gathered up in a knot there in the kind of misty half-rain. Smoke got pretty eloquent against my behalf.

"Point one is out of order," Professor Sampson says. "I have already accredited the team and admitted it to competition."

"Which case," Smoke says, "going elaborate on point two. Got the floor? Yeah, do? All *right*. Point is: not a gentleman. Redwine Walker. Busted me this morning, no reason. Just a rowdy. Been a rowdy all year. Depledged him from sacred Iota—"

All the non-fraternity boys gave a fat cheer and various bird calls and noises for old Smoke.

"Mr. Judge," he yells, and gets it quiet again, "*demand* ouster of captain, then. Without him, we drink against 'em. Huh? Fair? Sure! Walker not a gentleman, scholar. Huh? Ain't that right?"

"Are you a gentleman, sir?" Sampson says to me.

"I don't know, sir," I said.

The old sot called for some unbiased witnesses, then, and from the faculty, since it was a serious charge and a disqualifying one. He said he couldn't accept student views, because factions were evident.

It was fair enough, but I felt sure my hide was cooked, and it wouldn't be any pleasure for me if the independent team got somebody else and beat the Iotas. But Lucretius Finch steps out of the crowd, and gets quite an ovation from the students that have ever had him, and gives a bow and a broke-tooth grin around, and says Mr. Redwine Walker is perhaps not much of a scholar but that he had once declared definitely that he knew what constituted a gentleman and had never proved any different that *he* knew of, and said, what was a gentleman anyway? I saluted him.

"Yeah," Smoke Smith says, "gentlemen don't bring whores to Liberty Spring Retreat. Huh?"

That stung me; but Simon Arnold and Chaplain Erb had come wandering in, arm in arm, with their cheeks real pleasant, like they might have had a nip or two of something more than tea, and Simon Arnold says there are, in any situation, certainly in this one, certain words a gentleman doesn't use in public, and that Smoke Smith has just used one, he didn't know with what justification, but that he should be ashamed, instead of trying to shame Mr. Walker's date, who was probably a pure enough young damsel, judging by certain Spring Retreat standards he had seen operative at Liberty during the 200 years or so since he had been there. And Chaplain Erb jumps in and declares that I am not only a gentleman of the old school now rarely seen but that I am one of the leading Bible scholars to his knowledge, and winks at me, and I am sorry I never got that paper in to him, and sorry I ever told him to go to the bad place.

That swung it, and we went to the post, still under protest by Iota.

And, Iota finished first. They bent down to that table and one, two, three, and *zot*, they spilled that beer back over their shoulders and came up about a mile ahead of us, even though P.J. sucked his down at about Mach 125. Smoke leaps up on the table waving a mug like they were the winner, and I sprung for him to pull him down; but Sampson got in front of him and sticks up a hand and yells, "Cease!" He disqualifies the Iotas and we win.

It split the old Retreat right down the center, that little contest, it was the only time a fraternity hadn't won, and they were sore; but all the others were jubilant, and there were a lot more of them. I made a speech then and invited all of them to the party I was giving, and they all cheered. Of course, mine was only one of about 800 parties going on, and not all of them came, but about 100 did, and dates, and it was a swinging party, spread out all over our part of the dorm.

In town I gathered up Vera and a couple more cases of gin, and went back and had the party. Vera wore that sackified gray dress and stashed a suitcase under my bed with her outfit for later. She stood like a board and didn't speak to anybody, except to Anne, Dick's girl, that was awful nice to her and she said yes and no to her. She stood with a drink in her hand and flat-eyed the people that flowed in and out, and never put it to her bright lips. She was made up like a peacock, blue eyestuff and rouge and lipstick and orange fingernails and orange toenails through split high heels. She was a doll.

P.J. came to the party, and Mrs. P.J. Mrs. P.J. said, "How do you do, Redwine?" Rojo came over with a high-school girl he had. Slugger came in at last, like he promised, and says, "Aren't you a little young to be drinking martins, my good man?" I was mixing them 9 to 1, and his date had to help Slugger finally back down the hall to the Iota suite. It was a good party.

Bo didn't come to it. I went to see him and he was lying on his bed listening to songs of the fantastic fifties on the radio and he had shook Gee awake and was making him get ready for the evening, and told him not to come back in the room till he was through partying. He said he was going to lock the door and let the stupid debauchery roll around him.

"Come on, and have just one little martin with us, hoss?"

"No, Redwine. Thank you. I just want this damn thing over with."

"There's some good times, boy. I wish you'd had your girl come—"

"So we could double?"

"Okay," I said. "I'll be seeing you."

"I'll see you," he said.

Dinner was served at 6:30. After that there was supposed to be a period of socializing and cocktailing and general hooray until the dance commenced, along about ten-ish, like they said. The dance was in the auditorium. They had all the seats moved out and balloons and junk strung in there. They had hired Cool Deuce and the Diamonds to come in from the Red Lattice and play for the dance.

All the boys brought their dates to dinner, all that could make it, and they were dressed from formals to bathing suits. Chow was staked out on the long polished wood tables and they had candles flickering on them in old unpolished silver candleholders. That was all the light, and the clatter was terrible, and the shadows playing on the high walls and across the ceiling beams were weird. Me and Vera sat at a table with a motley bunch of boys, and most of them didn't have dates. The big hall was jampacked, so you were elbow in the next one's soup. We had a real meal that evening: game hens, and casseroles of this and that, and hot breads, and jellies, and fruit, and tomato aspic salad, and black olives and ice cream and cheeses and nuts, and they tried to float the hall in coffee, which wasn't a bad idea.

Some of the Delts got to tossing nuts at one another, and then they let fly a banana or two at the Sigs; and then there commenced a flying fruit war; and Monkey hops up, real desperate, and rings a huge cowbell he had to keep attention, and points to Rojo, who is song leader of the Iotas now, and the Iotas save the day by launching off into the songs. It was a good dinner, I enjoyed it, but Vera didn't eat; and one girl got a little sick in her lap at our table, and one old boy passed out clutching a hen leg; but it was pleasant enough.

> "Oh, hoist around your girdles
> And dig for your pads—
> Make way, lovely maidens,
> For the Liber-ty lads!"

Chaplain Erb was in his cassock and he gave the most intense kind of a grace to start it all off. Then when the nuts were cracking and the coffee was generally slopping throughout the hall, Monkey leaps up and clappers the bell. He stands at the head table and raises his arm for silence, and gets a hell of a hand.

"Hurrah for Monkey!" everybody shouts, and Rojo jumps up and leads us all in

> "Down in jungle town a honeymoon is coming soon.
> You can hear a ser-en-ade
> To a pretty mon-key maid,"

and Miss Pigeon, sitting next to Monkey, blushes, for that is the college's love song for those two. Finally he gets it half quieted down.

"On this wonderful occasion," he says, "fraught with traditional meaning for all of us—the time of the Liberty year dedicated to forgetting the cares of the day—it is a hyperbolic honor to have several manic guests that I would now like to present to you, so that you can enthusiastically adumbrate them a few words."

You couldn't hear Monkey too well, with the hoop-de-doo from table to table, the girls cackling and squealing, and the individual fraternities deciding they would sing their songs. Monkey introduced the mayor of Olive Hill. After the booing stopped it was the turn of the fat bishop that had been there before. He gets up, taps his fingers on his tummytum and says "My children—" but just then the Taus decide to start

"The night that Paddy Murphy died,"

and that song took a time, and Monkey whanged the cow-bell, until he had it tamed to Babel again. Then he presented the guest of honor: Ebenezer Gee, the great-great-great-(I don't know how many)-grandson of the Ebenezer Gee that came out in the woods and founded Liberty College.

Ebenezer is an old man with white bushy hair that can't quite decide to take over his face. He is a fine old ancient man, once they locate him. He is over at the side of the hall, sitting at one of the student tables, and he is an Englishman, from England, that has come over to speak to us specially. We applaud and yell and rise up and sing the Liberty Alma Mater to show him how glad we are.

He gets up and clears his throat, and it gets real actually silent.

He has on a saggy tweed suit, with a vest, and he hauls out a watch and looks at it, and holds it up to his ear, and cranks it, and revvs up his throat, and says to us:

"Outside, it is distinctly raining. I despise the rain. What? Abhor it.

"It rained on me. Frightful business. I despise umbrellas, howsomever. Father despised umbrellas, too.

"Grandfather despised umbrellas. His father could not tolerate them. He most certainly could not, sir.

"Ebenezer Gee, founder of Liberty College—*despised umbrellas!*"

He collapsed down into the arms of a nephew sitting beside him, named Monroe Gee. He was bombed.

After dinner, everybody sang down the paths together and then broke up for parties or to get ready for the dance.

"I want to go to the Iota party," Vera said.

"Already been a fracas with that bunch, missy."

"They have the best party," she said. "I've heard about the Iota Spring Retreat parties for years, Lord Liberty. Unless you're too damn chicken to take me.

"I can find somebody to take me," she said.

So we went. But first I collected Little Dick and Anne and Harmon Baumberg and his date, and Kingdom and the Ghana boy and his seven-foot buddy, a Gold Coast prince, and all the guys I knew from the Womb, and Gee and his old uncle, until there were about 50 of us; and then I thought they'd have a hard time doing anything.

Still, we were as welcome as the plague.

We flooded into the Iota suite and I thought the Bull would bust right off the wall and trample us. But they were too smart for that, and all kinds of folks were in there already, and it was open house all over, and Turk Randy came forward and said that we were welcome. Then they concentrated on Vera and me.

"Welcome," Slugger says. He turns to his date. "Honey," he says, "this is my dear ex-fraternity brother Redwine Walker. And have you met his date? Miss McAdams, Miss Whale. Miss Whale is the lovely dessert girl in the Olive Hill cafeteria."

"And the midnight snack girl in Liberty," Vera snarls to Miss McAdams. "Pleased to have met you, *honey*."

Vera moves over by Randy's Hawaii blond, blowing cigarette smoke up in her face.

"Ask Turkey who is the best," Vera tells her.

I pull her over to a corner and try to calm her down.

Randy comes and taps me on the shoulder, and we go down the hall and talk.

"Friend," Randy says, "I think you are the rottenest kind of a son of a bitch for dragging that hunk of human garbage in here. But you were determined. Okay, big man. Now, don't go for that belt. I don't want anything from you, or her. You got your taste, I got mine. I always like the Whale, she's fine in certain scenes. But this is my fiancée here, see? This is the Spring Retreat, see? The tradition says we got to welcome everybody tonight, but not you two. We got a whole fraternity here, ace. You want to see all these spooks and fags you brought here get hurt? Well, if Vera ain't out of there in five minutes after we go back in, we're going to clear out our dates, and I don't care how many it takes, we're going to clean you, man, and run her back to town like the dirty Chink whore she is. Hear all that?"

"Yo," I said. I saw he meant. "I've proved my point," I said.

"You proved what a bastard you are."

I didn't swing on him, but went in and pulled the Whale out of there—she was telling some filthy story to a group of horror-struck Iota dates. I pulled her out of there and she left shouting obscenities at the whole suite.

Her eyes were unholy. I couldn't remember she'd drunk a drink yet. I dragged her to my room.

"Get ready," I said, and walked down to the head to shower and shave.

When I got back she was just standing there.

"Get ready," I said.

She flipped off her floppy dress and stared at me, still and cold and bare as dirty marble.

"Do your dance," I said.

She howled at me and when I tried to touch her she scratched a long sharp line in my face from my eye to my cheek that ran blood and I slapped her silly down to the floor.

She sat there cross-legged and looked at me with pure hate.

"Leave me alone, Liberty," she said.

"Go alone, then," I said.

"I will."

She would of. She was here now.

She sat on the floor, like a naked fountain statue, and her lip was bleeding, like my cheek.

I grabbed my clothes and went down the hall to dress, to Bo's room, and I knocked and called, but he was asleep or he meant it for sure, he didn't open up, and I went to the john and dressed, and threw Vera a cold rag in my room, and then she locked herself in there, and dressed for an hour.

Consequently we were late. About eleven, and didn't get to see Monkey and Miss Pigeon lead off the dance in an old-fashioned waltz.

But when we arrived, everybody saw us.

They whispered, and oohed and aahed, the dancing slowed down to slow motion, and there came whistles and cat-calls and yells, and Vera Sevra was really the center of it, and the queen, from then on.

We made a pair. I wore a powder-blue tux with a red sash and tie and sharp-toed black and crimson boots. Vera came in on my arm, and she had used all that hour. She had made her face into a bright orange and yellow mask, so only the black oblong eyes showed what her face might really be. Her hair was greased and shining and piled up on her head and stuck through with a green jade comb. Bangles hung from her slit ears to her shoulders. The orange toes showed through the shoes.

It was the dress you saw. A look told you it was all she had on and it was white silk, stiff and painted on her, and cut without a back at all; and it was cut like a halter in front, with a strip of white silk covering each breast and cut on down to her belly-button, which was large and spongy.

I danced one dance with her, and then she pushed me away, and took the hand of one of the stags and made him dance with her. She did a cha-cha with Cristóbal Gottlieb that was obscene. Cool Deuce and the Diamonds got in the spirit, and began playing for her, and it got faster and faster and hotter and more exciting; and the Whale went crazy, dancing; and the boys went wild to dance with her, and picked her up and spun her around, and she never stopped, but started howling as she danced, and at the intermission led one of the Diamonds out and had him dance with her, without music. I jerked her away, she hissed at me but came over and stood against the refreshment table and watched them drink rum punch out of a tremendous carved-glass bowl.

"I want to swim in that," she said. When the music started I grabbed her hand and tried to dance with her, but she wrenched loose and found another partner. I started in on punch.

She had an effect on the other girls. Their dates would leave them and stand in line to dance with Vera. It wasn't nice to see how the boys stared at her, and left their dates, and then what the girls resorted to to keep their dates' attention.

Vera was swaying back and forth with Zambolatti, the seven-foot Gold Coast prince.

"Make him go," she told Zambolatti, and the giant let go of her and took hold of me and swung me around like a rag-doll so I landed on the floor.

"You're on your own," I said.

"Goodbye, Little Lord Liberty," she called, all the makeup on her face run together in a crazy blotch now and orange staining her teeth and her eyes glittering, dancing with that black tree. "Thanks *so* much."

She laughed.

Back in Liberty, in the Womb, I found Baumberg playing flute, and I got my horn. During that session I emptied my flask, and looked, and it was 1 a.m. I went up to Top Floor and things were full steam. In the Iota rooms Smoke was out of his mind, only he knew me. He came over. "Where la

169

Whale?" he said. "Huh? One man, not enough. Poor bastard. Redwine. Slugger, Redwine good old boy, huh? Sure. Stupid, simple—" I ducked when he smashed his mug at my head and shoved him over on the couch, where he lay passed out. A bunch of them were out of gas like that, boys and girls. Slugger was. "What am I supposed to do?" his date said. She was Miss McAdams, and was a cute girl with a short boy's haircut and drinking a gin drink. "I've got some gin in my room," I said, and took her hand, and led her down the dark hallway to it. On the way we had to step over a couple.

"Excuse me," I said.

"Goddamn you," the boy said.

"Oh, come *on*," the woman said. It was Mrs. P.J.

In my room we had a little surprise, as Dick and his Anne were in there.

"Sorry," Little Dick said. "We thought we could get away from the noise for a minute." They were sitting holding hands. "Horsehead's asleep."

So we sat and talked to them, and then Miss McAdams said she had to run along and see about Slugger, and I saw her later with a Low Floor boy.

"How's it go?" Dick said. "Where's Vera?"

"I'm sorry," he said. "How did you think it would be?"

"I thought—fairly decent. She said it would. I promised her, you know."

"Sure," Little Dick said.

"I don't know anything about it," Anne said, "but I feel sorry for that poor girl. My goodness, when you came in to the dance . . ."

"Yo," I said. "Well, be good. Stay as long as you like."

"I'm going back to the inn in a little while," Anne said.

It got pretty bad, in those early morning hours. The dance broke up, and Cool Deuce brought his music into Old Liberty. I couldn't find Vera. I was ready to hit sack, and knocked at

Bo's door again, but all the knocking in the world couldn't wake Bo when he was asleep. Downstairs I found P.J. and Spicer and his date.

"Seen the wife?" P.J. said. "It's getting along."

"Not for a while," I said.

"Hey there, Texas," Gretchen said.

"Hi," I said.

She smiled at me.

"You seem to have misplaced your date," Spicer said, smoking a cigarette in a holder and nervous as a cat. "I was *so* impressed with her at the dance."

"Oh, Michael," Gretchen said, "would you be the sweetest boy and go get me a scotch on the rocks while I go to the little girls' room?"

"I just tried, Gretchen dear. They don't have any scotch in here. Why don't we go to my room, and—"

"No," she said, and kissed his cheek. Those debutantes. "You run over to the next party and get your Gretchen some scotch. Michael?"

He padded off like a little white dog.

"You see the missus, tell her I've gone home to check the kiddoes," P.J. said.

Gretchen went on her mission, and I met her coming out. She grabbed my hand.

"He's getting that terrible nervous fidgeting," she said. "What do you call it, Redwine? The Horny Bird?"

She led me down the hall away from there, and we headed for Top Floor and stopped and I kissed her hard up against a door.

"You didn't even write, you wicked bastard," she said.

I took a chance and went to my room. It was free. Outside it had stopped raining and was bright and clear now, and I turned off the lights and put a record on and threw the drapes wide open for the moon.

"Bourbon do?"

"Yes."

"When are you and Socrates getting married?"

"September, I guess."

She drank the Jack Black I poured in her glass.

She eased on the bed, in an ice-blue formal that didn't suit her eyes and hair. She was a big girl, for Spicer to have.

"It's comfy here," she said.

"How are things in Hog Wallow, or that place you told me about?" she said.

"Shut up," I said.

"Red*wine*," she said, debutante as hell.

Gretchen was still a loving girl. But she liked to talk, and to talk about it, what you were doing at the moment, and to discuss if it was all right, and it could drive you *loco*. In about half an hour the ice-blue was off, but ever so slow, and I was telling her about the Kinsey Report and all like that, and she was saying no and all like that, and she had begun to tremble, and Rojo walks in.

"A-hem," he says.

She flung around and buried her face.

"Better be interesting, friend."

"Yes, man. Not to alarm. Oh, no. But Sister Whale, you know? Has ensconced her little self in the Womb. After a bath in the punch bowl at the dance, sans exotic costume. And— is kind of wild over there, and quite a few of the chaps around—

"*Amigo mío*," he said. "Thought you should know. Good-bye," he said.

"What is it?" Gretchen turned back and grabbed me.

"Have to leave."

"Don't," she says, cool as slow jazz. "Just when I've decided."

"Go calculate with Spicer," I told her. "I'm sure he would appreciate it."

In the Womb I found a gang of guys crowding around outside a door on third floor. I opened the door and went in the room. She cursed me when she saw me, and I left. She was receiving tribute from that tremendous prince; as I walked on down the hall I thought I heard a little wild cry and I thought, maybe he was the one. Then, I left there. I saw the big milk tub set out on the hill ready for the stuff to be poured in it, and the stars got dizzy. I dug out for Olive Hill. The night was dark but clear, I lurched through it in the buggy, buzzing with liquor and—*despair,* and busted up on to Marcy Lou's front porch, and rapped the door, finally the lights turned on, her father came and opened the door.

He was a fine, stern man.

"She went to Clayburg for the night," he said. "Do you know it's four o'clock?"

"Yes, sir," I said, staring at him.

"She's not here," he said. "She's just not here."

I drove around till the sun began to light up the sky with a promise of a beautiful day. It was very bright toward Liberty. It was too bright. A terrible ball of red and orange came on the horizon there, and it was separate from the sun. Black wisps of smoke rose up from it into the gray-blue sky. I gunned her fast as she could take the road, it was only minutes before I was there, but Old Liberty was already half burned down.

Chapter Twenty-Three

NOBODY knows why or how the fire started, but it began in the Womb and spread both ways. When I got there, it was a holocaust. That is the only word. Old Liberty was shredding its guts in belches of smoke and fire and collapsing wood up into the morning sky. The old observatory was gone from the center of the building. The Womb was a roaring inferno, flames were licking their orange tongues all along the building. Spews of smoke came out windows and shot from the Cyclops eyes of the towers. Boys shouted and screamed, and girls shrieked horribly. The ground in front of Old Liberty was like ants with people. I saw things falling out of the top and second and third story windows on both ends of Liberty, they were boys and girls jumping. The screams and smoke and heat were terrible. I stood frozen for a minute. Then I raced for our side.

I saw some folks hanging out a window on Top Floor where we lived, and they would hold on to this one boy hanging from the window ledge and then jump onto some mattresses somebody had set up. That one boy kept hanging there, passing them down. He must of handed down six or eight, so they could jump—then a beam fell, or something, and hit that boy, and you could hear his yell above all the rest, and it was a hunk of metal and wood from the top gutter that hit him, and it smashed his hand where he was holding on to the ledge, and severed off his fingers.

I fought my way over there to the mattresses to where that boy fell, and before I got there a girl in a flaming evening dress jumped from the second floor, screaming, and never had a chance to hit any mattresses and fell like a torch and crumpled up on the ground. I heard sirens now; they kept carrying them off to put in ambulances, and after the fire had only been burning forty minutes, the fire department chugged in from Olive Hill.

The boy that had been holding on to help the others out from Top Floor was Monroe Gee. He had passed down Spicer, and his date, and Slugger, that was lying peaceful-drunk and passed out on the charred grass now, and he had gone back in and found Baumberg and helped him get set to jump, and Little Dick. He was writhing on the ground, and his hand and arm were a nasty black-bloody pulp. I shook him. "God, Goddamn, God, God, God," he moaned.

"Bo?" I said. "Where's Bo?"

"He wasn't there," Baumberg said. "We looked—"

"The door was *locked*—"

"No—no—it wasn't—"

Little Dick was running frantic through the crowd. Monkey had started a bucket brigade—they were using buckets and glasses and beer mugs and spoons, I guess, to pour drops of water along from the nearest buildings to Old Liberty, and she was just lapping up the water grinning with hideous flame and smoke.

"Have you seen Bo Duddley?"

But it was too mixed up.

"For Christ's sake," somebody yelled at me. "Help with this water—"

I passed buckets along. The Olive Hill fire fighters ran

around in circles—there was only one hydrant for their hoses that worked by Liberty, down at the end of a long path. At last they got hoses run together and were able to stand and squirt one little flash of water on that huge boiling ball of flame and it disappeared in there with hardly a hiss.

They carried Turk Randy's girl with her clothes blackened on her and her face kind of dissolved in fire, and emitting a little horrible squeak to a car. All the girls from the inn and the boys that hadn't been in Old Liberty massed in front of the great burning building; and the police came to try to push them back, and a horde of folks from Olive Hill came and clogged the roads and paths all around, so they couldn't get the ambulances out, or the burned kids to cars, or the doctors and nurses in, and Randy's girl sat and died in a traffic jam on the road, for one.

When I ran around a policeman—"Everybody's out," he shouted at me—all of Low Floor was pure rolling smoke and licking flame. Clothes and all sorts of stuff were laid out in the hallways, that the boys had hoped to move out of there, and a lot of stuff was in the way. I could barely make it up to second floor and I found Horsehead staggering around up there, but I didn't see anybody else—windows kept popping out all over, and doors would just explode out from the force of the fire and it had spread through the Womb to the top of Old Liberty, and I had Horsehead's hand and we tried to make it up another flight, but the stairs had burned away, and I almost passed out from the smoke and fumes, and it was just impossible. We fought our way back down, and found a girl in an open first-floor room collapsed with not a mark on her, and I carried her down, and led Horsehead out all right. It was Mrs. P.J. and she was dead as a mackerel with her eyes popped open, had breathed in the smoke. She was in the room of a blind music student, but he had made it out all right.

Soon as I let Horsehead go, back outside, he got crazy. " 'ig, 'ig," he gurgled and shook loose from someone and went sobbing back in that blazing hell when he couldn't see Little Dick. Only Dick was out all right, of course, I'd told Horsehead that, Dick was looking for Horsehead. They had to hold Little Dick then on the ground to keep him from running in after Horsehead, when he knew it. That was just before the whole thing crumpled in. It went like a rocket disintegrating on the launching pad. It buckled from the towers on down. It got Horsehead.

Little Dick was kneeling on the grass, crying, and saying, in a trance, "*Thy* will be done . . . *Thy* will be done . . . Thy will . . ."

And the whole dormitory shuddered and went, and you could see new spouts of red and yellow flame shooting up and it grew to be twice as bright as before, and horribly hot, and then it settled down to serious, steady burning, and it was obvious it was going to be gutted now.

Horsehead was about the last tragic or desperate thing that happened, there. Someone got to me finally to tell me Bo had jumped pretty much at the start, and had been pretty broken up, and they had rushed him to the hospital in town. They were getting them all there by now; and everybody was simply standing watching Old Liberty burn, for it wasn't going to spread.

I hitched a ride with a car with some burned and sobbing girls in it, and it took 10 minutes to get a mile on that road. Most of the traffic was from town as folks came to watch the fire burn or to see the dead bodies or watch people die, I guess. So I jumped out of that car, and ran, and ran all the way to the hospital.

The hospital was jammed with folks. They were bringing doctors and more nurses in, but still a lot of them that had been hurt less bad had to sit and wait in the halls. Some parents, that lived close around, were already there, and they were weeping and gnashing. Of course the TV and newspaper boys were shooting away, and trying to keep the corpses and worst-burned ones in their pictures so the public could enjoy the tragedy to the fullest. Other parents, and the parents of the poor girls that had come to the big Spring Retreat, kept coming in and shouting for their kids, and they kept arriving in Olive Hill, but it took some of them a while. Olive Hill didn't have an airport.

Down one medicine and fire-stinking corridor I found Bo laid up in a room, all burned and broken up inside; they had strapped him to the little narrow bed, so he wouldn't thrash around. He lay jerking back and forth, he wasn't really conscious so he could recognize you in the least, but he never quit moving and I gave up trying to hold him still. I sat there about half an hour. It was one of those narrow rooms in that hospital; Jesus was hanging from the wall, white and full of pain.

Bo died quick after I got there, lying on that bed, tied down, with his insides busted, and they hadn't done much but inject stuff into him, and he shouted words I didn't know he knew. When he had died, I still sat there with him and Jesus; then a big nurse came and pulled me out of there pretty rough, and it was Mrs. Sevra; and I let her shove me into the corridor, and I never spoke to her, or her to me.

I wandered up and down the hallways for a while.

I found Gee on a cot near a dozen other burned boys, and his hair was all singed off and his eyebrows too, and he had unguent smeared all over, and was nursing his white-wrapped hand.

He was sober as I was, that was funny, to see him sober. I told him Bo was dead.

"I tried to find him," Gee said, and broke down, and I said, "Here's a cigarette, Monroe," and lit him one.

In another corridor I found the Whale. She was sitting propped in the hall with a lot of other girls hurt in the fire. She saw me coming, and tried to move away, but her leg was all wrapped up, and I could see it hurt her pretty bad. She looked terrible, burned on her face and arms, and she was sitting wrapped in somebody's overcoat, they must of found her naked as I left her. Her oblique metal eyes looking at me were hard and black. She cringed like a cur dog when I stopped in front of her, like she knew I was going to smash her.

But I didn't smash the Whale. I looked at the poor creature huddled there. Pretty soon I said, "It's all right, Vera. You can't help it, being the Whale. Who can help it? It's all right, girl."

I left her sitting in a hive of crying, shocked, and suffering girls and boys, and left her calling for me to come back; "Redwine, Redwine," she cried.

I walked to Dutch's. It was deserted but for Dutch, that was wiping glasses. I drank hot raw rye; somebody was chording "Lullaby of Birdland" on the juke.

Dutch wiped. "You smell like fire," he said. "You look like hell. You better go to the hospital."

"I been," I said, and left.

God Almighty, it was a glorious spring morning, full of blue sky and sun and light. I trudged on back to Liberty. It wasn't as conglomerated now; a lot of folks had left; Old Liberty had given over belching flames and was burning deep in her guts now, the towers and the whole center were gone, burning down to the foundation.

A collection of Liberty people, faculty and boys, were standing back from it. Spicer and Gretchen were there. She was talking a blue streak. "Have you seen Bo Duddley?" she said. I nodded. "Oh," she said, "thank *good*ness!" They were looking at the last body the fire fighters had gone in and found; it was under a shroud on the black grass and was the body of Abraham Lincoln Guznik.

> "Ah, sad and strange as in dark summer dawns
>   The earliest pipe of half awaken'd birds
>   To dying ears, when unto dying eyes
>   The casement suddenly grows a glimmering square;
>   So sad, so strange, the days that are no more."

Spicer spoke that, for Guznik, that wanted to be a poet.

We stood and looked at the body, and at the burning building.

"The Lord moves in a mysterious way?" Spicer said to Chaplain Erb.

The chaplain stared at it, at Liberty. "Hell, no," he said. "Not this. It was probably in the wiring." He flung his hands in his pockets under his robe and walked off just not quite as brisk as usual, toward the chapel.

"What will they *do?*" Gretchen said.

Nobody said anything.

"Why," I said, "build it back, I guess."

I sat up under a tremendous ash tree and slept a little bit. Later a two-engine plane came roaring in and bounced along to land on the football field. I had been waiting for it, and knew it would come. I stumbled down the hill to the field, and Bubba climbed out of the plane, and ran to meet me. Bubba put his arms around me, and led me to the plane; and we flew home to Javalina.

It was only after that, sitting in my Mama's spring garden, seeing the brilliant flowers blooming, that I could cry.

Chapter Twenty-Four

NINETEEN people were killed in the Liberty fire.

Besides Bo Duddley and Horsehead and Mrs. P.J. and Abraham Lincoln Guznik, six from the Womb died, the little happy boy from Ghana, and Henry Barnes got killed, a boy that never left his room on Low Floor. Three visiting girls died from jumping from windows or burning to death or suffocating in the smoke; and four more fraternity boys. And old Gilly, the janitor, got caught in it, and died. They found his lump of a burned body later, and that leg of his wasn't ivory, it was wood. But I was at the ranch.

For a week I sat and slept around the ranch. Until most of the singed hair grew long enough to cut and the burns on my hands and face gave over hurting; and for another week I went and worked sheep, with Uncle Sweet, in Mexico. I worked hard and concentrated on the work, so that evenings I would bulldog the jeep back to the quarters so beat and worn down I would drop into my bunk, and pass into sleep without a thought at all, except that I was aching for rest.

Or, sometimes, I would get a strong horse and ride, and ride all day in the wind and sun; and let the thrill of the gallop, and the sound of the horse pounding on the loose white stone and the jar of the horse and me together, and the burn of the sun and choke of the dust, and the sound of wild birds or a bobcat yelling, be it; and ride forever, and stop where I wanted, or go on into the night, and then, when I couldn't go any more, stop, and build a fire, and roll up to sleep by it, under the royal blue sky.

In the second week there, I received a letter forwarded to me from Javalina, and it was from Bo Duddley's father.

It said how glowing Bo had mentioned me in his letters, and how they looked forward to having us both there that summer before we came down to the ranch, and how excited Bo had been about it. Mr. Duddley said he and Mrs. Duddley and Bo's sister would appreciate it so much if I could come on sometime in the summer and visit them anyway, because, he said, they wanted to know Bo's friend, and it would be good for Bo's mama, since maybe she could unloose then and talk and weep about it some. He wrote that they had had the funeral, and more than 200 of the kin had come from around there to it, and they had tried not to make it too sad. He said I would like to see the beautiful place where Bo was laid to eternal rest.

In a day or two I managed to shoot back a note to the Duddleys, the best of a letter that I could: it thanked them, and said I couldn't visit them this summer, but I wanted to, sometime.

I went back to Javalina, and spent a couple days in our cabin along the river with a little Mexican maid we had. Only I woke up one day, still groggy from rum, and staggered out and jumped in the river six or seven times, and made a pot of black boiled coffee, and shaved, and then went to see my Daddy, *el hombrón*.

"I guess it's about time, now, to lay off foolishing and go back," I said.

"It is," Daddy said.

And so I did, and took the longest, slowest, creepingest drive back, and I passed through a small town, and stopped for a minute in a little plot thick with trees and flowers and grass, and found a wild bunch of holly down by the river and placed it there, and motored slowly out of there, and out of Indiana.

At Liberty they were carrying on, finishing the semester, such as it could be. They held classes, mere handfuls of students and the professors in the other buildings, or many times under the trees or walking on the paths. They ate the same gravied meat in the dining hall of mahogany and stone, and Monkey sat silent and smoked chains of cigarettes, and never ate, and no songs were sung.

THE END

This has been a kind of raggedy, strange story, I know, and I am sorry for that. It has merged together for me now, so it hardly makes sense. If I had waited another year to write it down, it might of come out clearer. I would be a sophomore, then.

Maybe there will be a new Old Liberty here by then, for I hear they will try to build it back stone on stone, just like it was before. It won't really be the same old monster, of course, and it will be strange and queer and hard to live in it at first. But maybe it will be all right. I went over there, to it, to where the ruins were yet smoking, and found old Finch and Simon Arnold there, looking at it, and Lucretius Finch kicked at the smoking stones of the foundation and at the charred wood and the ashes and black lumps in there, and said, "By Zeus." "By Zeus," he would say, and nod his head, and kick at it with his baggy old britches-leg.

"Mr. Walker," Simon Arnold said to me, "just now and musing here, I have composed a scrap of verse, my second poem and my last.

> Though Liberty may sometime burn,
> Old Liberty shall e'er return."

I don't know. A lot of the guys have not come back yet, and a bunch of them are transferring out. But Monkey's eyes are wild, and he exclaims there will be school here if with just five boys. Those that have stayed or come back now, Little Dick and Spicer and Gee and Baumberg and Smoke Smith and about 100, are living where they can, in Olive Hill or around. They tried to give Monroe Gee a national award for heroism in the fire, but he got drunk and didn't show up for the ceremony. I don't know what will happen to him, he lost those fingers on his hand, and can't make his little gesture to the world any more. He'll learn the other hand, I guess. I'm living in a tent I brought from home, and pitched it on the hill by Liberty, it suits me fine.

That's how it is right now, there are ten million stars out tonight, and I have got to go, and look for Marcy Lou, and quit this thing—I swear it was the best that I could do.

Well.

Goodbye, Bo. I'll be seeing you, old hoss.